CONJURING
THE INFINITE

Published by
Strident Publishing Ltd
22 Strathwhillan Drive
The Orchard
Hairmyres
East Kilbride
G75 8GT

Tel: +44 (0)1355 220588
info@stridentpublishing.co.uk
www.stridentpublishing.co.uk

Published by Strident Publishing, 2013
Text © Kirkland Ciccone, 2013
Cover art and design by www.LawrenceMann.co.uk

ISBN 978-1-905537-07-5

Typeset in Optima by oscarkills
Printed and bound by CPI Group (UK) Ltd, Croydon, CR0 4YY

The publisher acknowledges support from
Creative Scotland towards the publication of this title.

CONJURING
THE INFINITE
Kirkland Ciccone

www.stridentpublishing.co.uk

SETH KEVORKIAN RIP
The Funeral

The funeral of Seth Kevorkian was plodding along nicely until the solemn mood was devastated by a hideous scream.

The teenage residents of The Cottage watched with amusement as the source of the scream, a drunk, stumbled towards them with bulging eyes and mad flapping arms.

They hadn't expected *this* to happen at the funeral.

"Something's wrong with him," Lily announced, her flair for sarcasm in full flow.

Then as an afterthought she added:

"I hope it's something lethal."

Lily Myers was the youngest employee stationed at The Cottage. Despite her relative inexperience in the field of psychology, she constantly found herself being called upon by the others to enter into these sorts of situations. Nobody moved, not even Mother, except to send Lily 'the glare.' The glare was a silent command Lily knew only too well; this was her cue to do something before circumstances spiraled helplessly out of control.

There was a purposeful stride in Lily's step as she walked

away from the cluster of mourners. She crossed the cemetery with ease, reaching the screaming tramp in less than twelve footsteps. By her fifth footstep, Lily realised she recognised the man.

Coryn, one of the teenage housemates from The Cottage, watched events unfolding with interest. She uttered a silent prayer that the altercation would end violently for Lily. Perhaps the tramp could slap her across the face or give her a punt up the posterior. As long as the tramp did something...*anything*... to ruffle Lily's precious composure, that was fine with Coryn. She had nursed a violent dislike for the glamourous and bossy psychologist since the day Lily first arrived at The Cottage.

(Although Coryn didn't know it, her illogical dislike of Lily stemmed from bad experiences with other psychologists. It was a residue she couldn't clean from her mind.)

A whisper in Coryn's ear forced her attention away from the confrontation.

"Is she crazy?" Jack's voice said in awe. "She's actually squaring up to that dude!"

"That's because she's totally amazing." Coryn's words oozed with disdain.

The assembled teenagers and care workers watched and waited for the big bang.

Lily wasn't afraid of the noisy vagrant. She was standing in a public area with plenty of witnesses, so the man would keep his distance unless he was mentally unbalanced.

As a psychologist and employee at The Cottage, Lily had been taught to handle potentially explosive situations such as this, and her training certainly came in useful when dealing with people with emotional problems. She had also been hit with a few chairs in her time, which built up a kind of resistance to intimidating behaviour.

"What's wrong with you, Sam?" Lily asked in a soothing tone of voice, incidentally the same tone of voice she used when speaking to her cat Mr. Twiddles.

The name of the man causing the noise was Sam Carrickstone. The local townsfolk called him Soldier Sam because of his dirty brown army clothes. A strange, lost soul who drifted about town vainly trying to get people to pay attention to him, Sam wore nothing but army gear despite never having served in the army in his life. His clothes hadn't been washed in some time, a fact the cool breeze did nothing to disguise.

Lily felt physically ill due to the tangy odour of sweat and curry, but she quickly controlled her disgust and studied Sam with an objective unhurried gaze. She was distinctly unimpressed with the results of her flash assessment.

Soldier Sam's brown teeth bared themselves in a pained grin. His eyes, also brown, were full of unknown fright. His trembling hands ran through his greasy brown hair over and over again. Everything about Soldier Sam was brown and unremarkable. Lily would never have noticed him skulking around the graveyard if he hadn't started his outrageous screaming fits. In her professional opinion, Sam was suffering some kind of terrible mental assault. He had clearly suffered a mental breakdown, but he was also trying to get a message across, something that he couldn't say aloud because the words couldn't get past his screams.

"He's gone to Bournemouth," Soldier Sam finally said.

In the near distance, Coryn was straining to hear Soldier Sam's voice.

"What is he shouting?" Coryn asked the others. She couldn't understand him, because his speech was slurred. It sounded to Coryn like he was either drunk or on medication. Or both, she thought with amusement.

"He just mentioned Bournemouth," said Julee knowledgeably. Julee was one of the other residents of The Cottage and at fifteen years old was the same age as Jack.

Coryn flashed a look of mild dislike at Julee. Like Julee, she always seemed to get things right. Everything came effortlessly to Julee, and she always looked great no matter what happened; she even looked insufferably prim after brawling with the mean girls at school. Coryn, conscious of both her weight and unremarkable face, loathed Julee for many reasons, but the vital motivation for her dislike was a secret suspicion that Jack fancied Julee. Julee, however, either didn't know of Jack's interest in her or worse…she didn't care.

In the eyes of Coryn, this was the worst crime Julee could ever commit.

"Bournemouth?" Jack looked over at Julee with a bewitched smile.

"Bournemouth is hell."

Only Jack questioned Julee's rather odd explanation.

"How do you know that?" He laughed, despite himself.

"Someone told me," Julee replied, squinting at the grave in front of them. Jack, immediately aware who had told Julee about Bournemouth, said nothing more.

Regardless of the small distance between them, the group could see Soldier Sam was struggling to say something to a visibly indifferent Lily. At this point, Jack suddenly realised that he too knew the strange man standing in the near distance.

"What is wrong with you, Sam?" Lily really wanted to move this on. It was getting late and she didn't want to spend a full afternoon hanging about in a graveyard with a group of gawking teenagers.

"The eyes of the sky have opened," Soldier Sam snarled.

Lily automatically recoiled from the poison delivered in the strange words. Her head was already full of other troubles, mostly those from The Cottage, and a few from her personal life. Soldier Sam's cryptically creepy commentary was the last thing she wanted or needed to hear right now.

"Please..." Soldier Sam said pleadingly, "Seth's gone to Bournemouth!"

"I'm sure he has," Lily cooed gently, "it's probably really nice this time of year."

She couldn't think what else she could say, so she fell back on her training, eagerly agreeing with Sam's every word. Failure to do so might have resulted in more screaming and Lily didn't want another scene made at the service.

"I don't want to go." Soldier Sam's body was racked with dreadful sobbing. "He's going to come and get me and take me away."

"Take you away where?" Lily asked cautiously.

"He wants to take us all to Bournemouth!" Soldier Sam cried out.

Then the dreadful screaming started up again with a renewed intensity. Lily looked back at everybody surrounding the coffin; some seemed jittery and restless, whilst others appeared rather amused. She shrugged at them, her way of admitting defeat.

Two men, presumably the graveyard official and a co-worker, came over and hauled Sam away from Lily. The crowd from The Cottage, now satisfied they were safe from harm, quickly made their way towards her for an explanation.

The main service for Seth was over. All that remained was for everybody was to go home and remember Seth in their own personal way.

"Ashes to ashes, dust to dust," Coryn said bitterly as she left the graveyard.

There were seven visitors from The Cottage at the funeral. Three of them were the teenaged residents, while the other four — including Lily and Mother — came from staff.

A small coach had been provided by the local council at little expense, so seven passengers was a good small number to keep costs down further. The group headed towards the bus as soon as the funeral ended, all desperately wanting to get far away from the graveyard and further away from crazy Soldier Sam.

But Soldier Sam had plans of his own. The cluster of teenagers and Cottage staff had scarcely climbed into the modest bus when Sam suddenly appeared out of nowhere. He roared and gestured menacingly at everybody.

His hands were soaked in bright red blood. He smeared them against the windows of the coach. Then a mighty torment wracked his body and he started slamming his bloody hands against the glass with enough strength to crinkle the panes with cracks.

Lily's training hadn't prepared her for this level of insanity, so she backed away open-mouthed in horror. The others followed when they realised even the usually unflappable, permanently unflustered Lily was frightened.

"Get the hell away from us!" Julee cried out. "We're calling the police!"

Jack, the tallest teenager at the funeral, eventually decided that enough was enough. Bolstered by the thought of gaining Julee's admiration, he jumped out of the bus and pushed Sam away with real fury. It was a savage and sudden burst of violence from a teenage boy known for his impulsive rages.

"Remember me?" Jack whispered under his breath, out of the hearing of the others.

Soldier Sam did indeed recognise Jack from an earlier encounter. As a result, Jack's intervention was enough to scare him off. Sam turned and ran away down the road, his screams quickly fading into the distance.

Jack sighed with relief. Nobody knew what had taken place between him and Soldier Sam; only Seth knew what happened that day, but he was no longer in a position to tell the others.

Instead of dwelling on the past, Jack turned his attention to the others. He carefully studied the bloody palm prints dripping on the windows of the bus.

"It isn't blood," a relieved Jack informed Mother, "it's just red paint!"

Coryn was the first to see the enormous red words on the wall of the church. She read the message but she didn't understand the meaning. Nobody did. As the bus pulled out of the church car park, the words suddenly appeared before the window of the driver's seat so every passenger had to read them just as Soldier Sam intended:

SETH KEVORKIAN HAS GONE TO BOURNEMOUTH!

This was nonsense though. Everybody on the bus knew Seth was dead, even if the painted wall scrawl said otherwise. His own grandmother had identified his body two weeks ago. He had been shot in the chest at close range by a gun nobody could find.

Seth wasn't anywhere else except deep in the ground.

IN THE HOUSE WE CALL HOME
After The Funeral

The Cottage had once belonged to the owner of the nearby mines, during a time when coal had been essential in heating British homes. Those days had long passed and the mines now lay gutted and empty, dark and useless. Only The Cottage remained.

It wasn't really a cottage, not anymore, because large and ugly extensions had been grafted onto the original building like botched cosmetic surgery on an otherwise handsome face. What had started as a large family home had gradually evolved into a care facility for troublesome teenagers. Some of them didn't last long in The Cottage, while others couldn't last anywhere else.

The inside of The Cottage was an entirely different proposition from the outside. It was a luxurious complex where comfort and splendor were both considered essential parts of the therapeutic process. Mother had often argued that alternative therapy could only work in happy surroundings. As a result of this principle, each teenager living at The Cottage had their own bedroom; a private space they could relax within while they enjoyed the benefits of The Cottage's environment.

Each room was fully furnished with a king-size bed and an en suite bathroom complete with powerful shower and luxurious soaps and toiletries. For the convenience of the residents, rooms also came complete with storage space facilities for clothing. Curiously, a shelf of books crammed full of indispensable reading materials was also provided for the residents.

The common room came complete with widescreen plasma television and some gaming consoles. There was also a television in every bedroom and of course a Wi-Fi service easily accessible to everybody living in The Cottage.

It was the most wonderful place to live and for some, the most horrible.

The bus crunched noisily onto the gravel at the front of The Cottage, marking its territory in the car park. The passengers quickly descended. Their journey from the funeral of Seth had been quick and pleasant, but a profound sense of dread passed through everybody on their return home.

It was time to have a meal and think about Seth. Mother had earlier decreed that all occupants in The Cottage should attend the memorial dinner; it was her professional opinion that it would help them come to terms with Seth's death.

The astute housemates, however, used the journey back from the graveyard wisely. They thought up stories about Seth in case Mother insisted they tell lovely tales about him during dinner — stories that confirmed how wonderful Seth was while he lived and breathed, stories that established Seth as a hero, an all-round good guy.

The only problem was that their stories would be completely untrue. Why? Because the truth was that Seth Kevorkian was not a nice person. He was utterly unpleasant and everybody in The

Cottage knew this except Mother.

She was mourning for a boy who didn't exist.

When the residents returned from the funeral, they discovered a new addition to the grand hallway of The Cottage. A massive photograph of Seth Kevorkian had been installed during their absence and it effortlessly dominated the entire hallway.

It showed Seth's face, blown up to obscenely large proportions, smiling a gleefully counterfeit smile. Underneath the enormous portrait sat a wreath of delicately arranged flowers teased into a floral tribute that read NEVER FORGET.

"It's beautiful," Mother said mournfully as she paid her respects to the dead teenager in the photograph. It was her shrine to Seth, her favourite resident in The Cottage. Death had given him an inner beauty he lacked in life, this portrait was the realisation of Mother's imaginary vision of him.

"I think it looks like something out of a nightmare," Coryn whispered to Jack. He tried but failed to hide a smile. He agreed with her judgment.

"I never liked his name," Julee said abruptly.

"You didn't like his name?" This amused Jack, much to Coryn's exasperation.

"I think it sounded really sinister, didn't it? 'Seth Kevorkian.' It suited him. He could never have been called John Smith or something like that. Not with his temperament and personality."

Coryn grudgingly admitted to herself that Julee was right in her assessment. She suddenly found herself gazing longingly at Julee's beautiful blonde hair, wishing it would fall out onto the laminate floor.

"Let's head on through to the dining room," Lily said, naturally taking the lead.

The teenagers obediently filed into a line behind her and walked where Lily walked. Mother, being a creature of habit, had allocated each member of The Cottage household a specific chair of their own at the long table inside the dining room.

A tall hairless boy by the name of Lawrence soon entered the dining room and took a seat next to Coryn. He smiled anxiously and gave the others a cheery little wave.

Lawrence was one of the more recent housemates to move into The Cottage. He hadn't been at the funeral, having successfully faked illness to avoid attending. While alive, Seth had relentlessly teased Lawrence about his baldness. Nobody in The Cottage save Mother knew the reason for Lawrence's lack of hair, but he would invent explanations whenever someone was brave enough to ask him. Sometimes he blamed stress, another explanation placed the fault on a UFO, but Seth told everybody it was because Lawrence had a contagious disease.

Another gigantic photograph of Seth had been placed in the dining room.

"That's vile," Coryn said as her eyes fell upon the second framed monstrosity.

"Mother insists that it'll help the grieving process," Lawrence said with a wry smile. He'd just spotted the portrait and couldn't quite believe it was real.

"Mother talks a load of crap!" Julee snapped tetchily. The idea of having to eat dinner in front of Seth's face wasn't an appealing one. It freaked her out, actually.

"This we agree on," Lawrence chuckled.

"Julee's right once again," Coryn muttered quietly.

Lily caught onto Julee's comment and her reaction wasn't a favorable one. "There's no need to be disrespectful about Mother," she said tersely, while adjusting her chair. "It is customary at a memorial for pictures of the deceased to be featured."

(Although she would never admit it, Lily actually agreed with Julee's harsh assessment of Mother. The old bat really did talk a load of old toot at times.)

A small punky thing with an elfin face and a short black haircut to match entered the dining room and took a seat with the rest of them. This was Reet, full name Reeta. A timid but classy girl, her mother's rampant alcoholism meant that she had to be taken into care, eventually ending up in The Cottage. Every now and then, Reet's mother wrote to her from rehab, but the handwriting changed in every letter; Reet suspected her mother was getting someone different to write each month.

"Yuck," Reet grumbled as she caught sight of Seth's memorial portrait, "that is going to put me right off dinner!"

"It's not going to put me off mine," Lawrence said merrily.

Nobody knew how long Mother had worked in The Cottage, but she seemed to be part of the building's very fabric. Even the staff joked that it had been built around her. Not even Mother's real name was known so people called her 'Mother' as an affectionate nod to her status in The Cottage. Some cruel gossips joked that she liked the name because she treated the inmates of The Cottage as surrogate family.

Nobody, however, could ridicule the amount of effort she put into her work. Mother always got results through an unholy alliance of sweetness, determination and ruthlessness.

The techniques she deployed could turn the most aggressive and obstinate teenage tearaway into someone far greater and better. The people sent to The Cottage suffered from bad parenting; their parents were either in prison, rehab or (in the case of Seth's father) dead and gone. Mother's theory from this perspective was a simple one: Unstable teenagers will grow to be stable in a stable environment.

Seth had been Mother's favourite and everybody sitting at the table knew his death had hit her hardest of all. It was for that reason she intended the memorial dinner to go smoothly. His own family had failed him, but Mother would do him proud.

Mother sat idly, lost in her own thoughts, staring into space while the others chatted away quietly. Her advancing years meant she couldn't hear the whispers of the dinner guests, but she probably wouldn't appreciate what they were saying anyway.

She soon came out of her daydream and found Lily sitting beside her. Lily was young and perhaps one day she would be a worthy replacement to run The Cottage, but until then Lily had a lot to learn, and Mother felt she had a lot to teach.

The strange expression on Mother's face, caused by her deep thoughts, hadn't escaped Lily. The young psychologist leaned over and smiled warmly at Mother, trying to make her feel a little bit better, but totally failing.

"Are you feeling okay?"

"Yes," Mother replied, "of course I am dear."

Mother's eyes turned away from Lily and fell upon the portrait of Seth. She wanted to congratulate the artist upon successfully capturing Seth's inner sincerity.

"I miss him," Mother said softly.

Lily was touched by this rare display of emotion from the usually stern Supervisor.

"I miss him too," Lily lied smoothly.

The kitchen staff entered the dining room and efficiently started serving the first course of the memorial dinner.

"The servants are coming in with starters!" Coryn yelled enthusiastically. She was always excited when food came into close proximity.

Lily rolled her eyes at Coryn's blatant disrespect. She hated the kitchen staff being described as 'servants', she found it demeaning, and yet Coryn always insisted on insulting them. Lily decided to use her training to politely inform Coryn not to be so bad-mannered; Coryn was a classic case of a teen trapped in a cycle of endless self-loathing, she seemed to focus her insecurities on people she deemed inferior to herself. There was no way she would ever dare insult someone like Julee, so instead she focused on kitchen porters, bin men, teachers and other people with 'lowly' jobs.

"Coryn, don't speak to people like that. You might end up working in a kitchen."

Coryn shot Lily a truly vile glare. Lily knew fine well Coryn resented her as she did nearly everybody. But she couldn't bring herself to care, she wasn't officially on duty right now, in fact she was only attending this dinner at Mother's insistence. She didn't want to be part of Seth's memorial, but Mother could be very dogged in the pursuit of whatever she wanted. She had sweetly insisted Lily be there 'or else.'

Food suddenly filled the plate of the grateful housemates. The first course was a choice between minestrone soup or a lightly tossed Caesar salad with sun blushed tomato. No high-fat microwave meals at The Cottage, it only employed the finest chefs in the district.

"I want you all to think about Seth," Mother said quietly as she speared a lettuce leaf with her fork.

"We could tell stories to celebrate his life."

Coryn wasn't listening though; she was busy with a bowl brimming with soup. She was hungry and hadn't eaten properly all day. Her fingers clumsily tore at some bread and she furiously dipped a chunk into her soup, dripping it everywhere.

Lily frowned in disgust. She couldn't stand girls who ate like pigs.

"The Abomination isn't down yet," Julee said cautiously.

"If you are referring to Patricia," Lily said sternly, using The Abomination's real name, "she's not coming down tonight. And please don't call her that name."

Everybody in the room breathed an invisible sigh of relief at Lily's statement; they were all nearly as terrified of Patricia as they had been of Seth. Patricia, another housemate in The Cottage, was mentally unhinged and frighteningly unstable. She hadn't been given her nickname without good reason.

Julee let loose a weary sigh, "What did The Abomin…Patricia do this time?"

Mother suddenly entered into the discussion:

"She attacked two members of my staff today and bit one of them on the leg. I will not have her causing a scene tonight. Seth deserves better than that."

Julee started on her Caesar salad, but even she had to laugh at Mother's delusions. Seth, when he had still been alive, had used Patricia as his muscle to beat people up if they did anything to displease him. Every few days, someone would be on the receiving end of her deranged rages, and that was usually as a result of Seth's exploitation. He couldn't fight physically, so he tended to manipulate from afar.

Lily, meanwhile, was reaching over towards a jug of water in close proximity. She lifted it and tipped some of it into a gleaming glass. She didn't even want to talk about Seth, let alone tell a whole story about him. It wasn't in her best interests to be that honest with the teenagers she was paid to help.

Suddenly Lily's gloomy mood lifted and twisted into joy as a new idea flourished in the recesses of her mind. She decided to thrust Coryn into an awkward situation, her petty revenge on the teenager who ate like a pig and openly insulted the care staff.

"Why don't *you* tell a story about Seth?" Lily eyed Coryn directly. She knew out of the housemates, it was Coryn who loathed Seth most of all, though only just.

Coryn suddenly appeared very nervous to the other dinner guests. Bursts of terror passed through Coryn as the others looked at her expectantly.

"I don't really have any stories about Seth," Coryn said with a quiver in her voice.

Reet and Lawrence suddenly broke the underlying tension by laughing loudly. Coryn had a horrible feeling she knew what they were laughing about, she even thought she saw Reet mouthing the word 'diary', but she pretended to be oblivious. Coryn's general paranoia made her suspect everybody talked about her constantly; indeed her mind had the amazing capacity to overhear people saying things about her when in fact they were discussing something completely different.

She glowered angrily through narrow eyes at Reet and Lawrence, quickly silencing both of them. They knew she could take them in a fight if she was angry enough.

"I would like to tell you all a story about Seth," Mother announced abruptly, "I'll tell you about my very first meeting with him. It wasn't long ago, so I still remember it vividly. That would be a nice way to kick start proceedings, wouldn't it? Yes?"

Coryn breathed an inward sigh of relief. Her hatred for Lily flared hotly but she also had a powerful urge to smack Mother in the face for dreaming up this stupid post-funeral dinner party. It took all of her self-control not to attack them both. She didn't want to end up like The Abomination, sitting in a room alone and sedated for her own safety, so she boiled silently in her own rage.

When Mother started telling her story, Coryn suddenly started fretting over hers.

NATURE, NURTURE, AND NONSENSE

Nobody is born evil. Bad people are influenced by their life experiences. Mother knew that the key to rehabilitating every lost teenager who passed through the gates of The Cottage was to understand what drove them to act destructively, only then could she successfully turn a delinquent into a productive member of society.

She had always prided herself in her ability to understand teenagers, to assess them with a mere glance. This wasn't difficult for Mother, because most teenagers tended to be the same, no matter which clothes they wore or what trends they followed.

But Mother soon discovered that Seth Kevorkian was not a typical teenager.

The first time she met him, he seemed delighted to meet her. That wasn't a normal reaction from new housemates. She couldn't remember the last time a resident seemed so happy to be in her company. She couldn't actually remember the first time! Most tenants in The Cottage tolerated or humored Mother. Her old age marked her out as irrelevant to the youthful mindset.

Seth was different. He wasn't the surly, grumpy, rude tearaway Mother had expected to meet. The reports she had been emailed were completely inconsistent with the boy in front of her. Mother preferred to make up her own mind anyway, so she decided not to pay any attention to the dire warnings of Seth's psychiatric assessments. Her intuition would be adequate enough.

They both sat there face to face, studying each other in an office thick with the sluggish heat of a July summer. Every new resident at The Cottage had to go through several rituals before settling into their routine. The first and most important of these rituals was an interview with Mother.

Mother liked to present an unruffled demeanor to her new tenants, but the heat was so oppressive that she found it almost impossible to look anything less than disheveled. Her graying hair fell limp and wet over her forehead. It did feel nice.

Seth, however, seemed totally immune to the extreme warmth.

"You're much younger than I thought you would be," he said with a handsome grin.

Mother felt a colossal but passing heave of joy blossoming deep inside her. Nobody ever complimented Mother on her appearance. She felt warmth flushing through her skin and she quickly turned away, hiding her face in a stack of files.

Mother decided to blame the sudden warmth on the summer heat outside.

"What is this place?" Seth continued wearily. "I feel like a yo-yo. I've been shunted back and forth between foster homes and orphanages. Is this a youth offender's institute? It isn't like the ones I've been in before. I hope you don't expect me to share a room with someone else, because I won't do it."

It was Mother's turn to speak now. She jotted down notes during the introductory interview and took the chance to look over her bifocal spectacles at Seth. He was well-groomed and clean, which wasn't always the case with new tenants of The Cottage. Mother sometimes despaired at how badly-dressed some teenagers were. This, in Mother's unspoken opinion, was the fault of lazy parenting.

"This is *not* a youth offender's institute. It is The Cottage. We take in troubled teenagers who have been abandoned in the system with nowhere else to go. Then we take and reshape you into better people so you don't end up like your parents. We only accept people with potential; teenagers we feel can contribute to society."

Mother was completely in her element now; Seth noticed how enthusiastic she was becoming as she launched into a feel-good speech about The Cottage.

"Our favourite word here, Seth, is the word *If*."

"*If?*" Seth said doubtfully.

"Yes. *If* is a short word but it is also incredibly significant. *If* you want to go out into the world as a better person, we can help you achieve that, but only *If* you help us to help you. You can do anything *If* you have the right tools in life."

Seth privately wondered whether he'd accidentally stumbled into a really bad comedy movie, but Mother sought to reassure him about The Cottage.

"I promise you won't need to share a room with anyone, so please don't get upset."

Mother initially felt Seth's subsequent laughter sounded slightly contemptuous, but she swiftly reassessed her opinion. When he spoke again, it was with a voice which held a sociable tone Mother didn't hear very often from the mouth of a young man.

"I'm glad. The Cottage is very beautiful. I'm looking forward to my stay here."

Mother decided to move the interview onwards and talk to Seth about his family. Unlike the other tenants whose parents were in jail or on the run from the law, Seth's actual mother was still alive and living a high-quality life. But she stubbornly refused to have Seth near her. The reports written up by the social workers stated that she seemed utterly terrified of him. Mother couldn't understand why anybody would be scared of someone as charming as the youngster facing her.

"Your father died quite recently according to your file. I'm sorry for your loss..."

"He wasn't a nice man," Seth said easily, "I'm over it. I'm made of tough stuff!"

Mother studied his face and couldn't tell whether or not he was being truthful. She had no idea what kind of person Seth Kevorkian really was, however she suspected that cracking his hard exterior would prove tough but ultimately satisfying. She had to ask a few more questions for the benefit of her files, after all, Lily would have to look through them and assess Seth during her own time.

"It must have been quite a shock for you to find his body."

Seth leaned back on his chair and pressed his fingers together, his face stony still. Thinking about his father's death brought unwanted memories to the surface. Mother felt a sense of sadness rinse over her, along with the slightest hint of regret. Sometimes being in charge at The Cottage meant asking the difficult questions.

"Can I ask how he died?" Mother asked in her most sympathetic tone of voice.

Seth's response was somewhat cryptic:

"He never got to his heart medication on time."

Mother turned away to get the box of paper tissues handily placed behind her on the windowsill. She turned back and thrust some tissues into Seth's hand, and he proceeded to wipe unseen tears from his eyes. Every now and then, he would cover his face and again his sobs would change into a noise that sounded uncannily like laughter. But Mother knew Seth couldn't actually be laughing. It was probable he was still deep in grief and hadn't totally processed his enormous loss.

"Let it all out," Mother cooed gently, "You aren't alone Seth, there are other people here like you."

"There's nobody quite like me," Seth replied in a voice that was positively arctic. Then he shielded his face with the rotted remains of his handkerchief.

"We have many people here in a similar situation to you," Mother replied, totally missing the thrust of Seth's statement. "Some of my teenagers have been abandoned by their parents. Some have parents in prison for drugs and other offences. There are also other reasons for some of my teenagers being here. Tact, however, doesn't allow me to divulge them to you. Perhaps one day they will tell you about their lives. Not all of their stories are pleasant. But the truth is always beautiful no matter how ugly the tale. My own mother used to say that to me. She was very plainspoken, indeed it was she who instilled in me a love for the word 'if'."

(Mother didn't catch Seth rolling his eyes at her arrogant speech.)

"Thank you for your generosity. I'm ready and willing to get stuck in now."

"I'm so glad you said that, Seth."

Seth rose up from his chair and smiled his version of a benign smile, an imitation grin, but it was enough to convince Mother. He then left the office and Mother was alone all over again.

She sat in silence for nearly twenty minutes, contemplating how different The Cottage would be now Seth had arrived. He was just what the place needed; a pleasant, friendly presence to galvanise the others with his innate thoughtfulness.

She had no idea she was already being swayed by a skillful manipulator.

If Mother had bothered looking at Seth's face as he left her office, she might have noticed a strange expression darken his features. If Mother had gazed deep into his eyes, she might have noticed a callous twinkle. If Mother had listened carefully, she might have heard his scornful laughter echo down the hallway. If Mother had trusted the reports in front of her instead of relying on her own instincts, she might have prevented the dark events that took place afterwards.

If.

GHOST STORIES
After The Funeral

Reet surveyed the dinner menu with greedy eyes. She impatiently pointed out what she wanted to eat, licking her full lips at the thought of gorging herself silly. She finally decided the Chicken Breast with Mushroom and Cream Sauce sounded rather enticing. Her choice of meal, however, provoked a bewildered response from the other housemates, but most shocked of all was Julee.

"You're a vegetarian. Have you forgotten already? Save the animals et cetera?"

Reet looked over at her friend and suddenly it dawned on her that Julee was right. Her face reddened and she changed her choice of meal, switching from the Chicken Breast to Mushroom Lasagna. She put the menu tentatively down onto the table only to see it snatched up by Jack, who was also looking forward to a big dinner.

Lily didn't take her eyes off Reet during the pre-meal conversation. Not even once.

Halfway during their main course, not long after her rose-tinted story, Mother had to abandon the table in order to deal with The Abomination. The care workers were always having problems with Patricia because it took nearly eight of them to hold her down whenever she freaked out. All attempts at moderating Patricia's behaviour were fast becoming more and more difficult. In the last few days, Lily had overheard various phone conversations between Mother and Patricia's parents. The walls in Lily's office were paper thin which meant privacy was nonexistent. Mother's voice sounded angry and frustrated, she complained about how 'inhumane' it was to continually medicate The Abomination, but the parents didn't seem interested in the fate of their daughter. They were probably grateful to be away from her.

The nasty sound of violence upstairs made everybody in the dining room pause nervously. The upstairs voices yelled for calm, but their pleas were unsuccessful. Nobody at the dinner table said anything, because they knew exactly what was happening, they'd all witnessed The Abomination during one of her psycho attacks.

"Let's just talk about Seth and shame the devil," Julee said abruptly.

"What do you mean?" Lily asked, relieved that someone had ended the uncomfortable silence. She needed a distraction from the distressing sounds upstairs. It dawned on her that perhaps she should have left with Mother, but she decided to remain behind and keep an eye on the others. She had a feeling their conversation was about to take a turn for the interesting.

"We shouldn't speak ill of the dead, but Seth was unbearable," Julee said.

Coryn nodded appreciatively, which was rare for her, but Julee had just said aloud exactly what she had been thinking earlier.

"Julee's right," Coryn agreed, "he was sick in the head. He should have been locked up for the things he got away with. You all know how much I hated him."

Reet laughed apprehensively. Lawrence, of course, followed her lead.

"He was a bit of an eccentric," Jack said in a tone that suggested he agreed but didn't want to admit it. "But he wasn't all bad. I got along with him okay."

"He freaked me out!" Julee said. "His interest in witchcraft was unhealthy."

"Weird stuff always seemed to happen around Seth."

Everybody at the table turned to look at Lawrence. They knew *exactly* what he meant. Lily's keen eye for detail picked up something between the teenagers; it seemed Seth's death had provided an excuse to finally open up and talk about it. An event they'd witnessed, an experience they didn't want to remember.

"Halloween?" Coryn replied with a trembling voice. "Please not Halloween."

"We all agreed never to talk about Halloween again," Reet said wearily.

"Talk about Seth and shame the devil, remember?" Julee said quietly. "He's dead anyway, so I hardly think it matters if we talk about what he did to us on Halloween."

Lily finished off her dinner with great gusto before leaning in towards the teenagers, eager to hear exactly what they were discussing. Mother's hasty departure and the fine dining provided to them had evidently caused the housemates to relax. They were beginning to open up about Seth now. Lily found that her presence made no difference whatsoever, a sign she took to be a good one, because it meant everybody living at The Cottage saw her in a more favorable light to Mother.

"Quite right too," Lily muttered to herself.

All eyes looked over at her, suddenly aware an outsider was listening to their whispered conversations. Lily decided to take charge of the situation and in her usual forthright manner, she asked one simple question:

"What did Seth do to you on Halloween?"

Nobody replied at first until Julee spoke out. Lily had known it would be Julee.

"He tried to Conjure The Infinite on Halloween."

Coryn shrieked like a terrified child before accidentally knocking over a glass of water poured by one of the staff. Lily noted with disapproval that the portly girl blamed the unlucky help for her own mistake — but something Julee said had obviously frightened the girl. It wasn't only her though. Three simple words like 'Conjure The Infinite' noticeably unnerved everyone at the table. There was clearly something in the meaning of the phrase that had brought about a terrible silence only Lily dared to break.

"I don't have a clue what you're all on about. What does this have to do with Seth's death? What exactly is this 'Infinite' anyway?"

Julee smiled an empty smile.

"It's a ghost story, a legend, a fairy tale, a spooky yarn. That's all."

HALLOWEEN

"The Infinite is an entity from the higher dimensions," Seth explained warily as he led everybody towards the forest. "It rules over a vast kingdom of magick, and it seeks a worthy servant to imbue with equally vast supernatural power."

It was precisely that part of Seth's explanation that Jack found confusing. Seth had explained the story three times, but Jack was the only person in the group who didn't seem to get it.

"Why would The Infinite want to give anyone that kind of power?"

He could almost hear the sound of Seth rolling his eyes. Seth did this quite often.

"I've already told you," Seth said evasively, "The Infinite seeks ways to enter into other dimensions. It can't just access this realm at will, it has to be invited by one of the initiated, and that's exactly what I intend to do tonight: invite it. Then The Infinite will come and take me far away from this dump."

Coryn's heart quickened with joy at Seth's words, because she really did wish something…anything….would come and deposit him in a distant country, but she never said this aloud to anyone, because her wishes never came true.

"Happy Halloween, folks!" Julee's voice drifted across the

night.

"Happy Halloween!" Seth mimicked Julee's boisterous tone perfectly.

The housemates of The Cottage had climbed out of Reet's window over an hour ago as part of a Halloween dare to sneak into the scary forest which surrounded the village. Seth quickly seized upon the opportunity to try and cast some spells, and even though none of the others took his witchcraft mumbo jumbo seriously, they all agreed that it sounded like a cool thing to do on Halloween.

"What happens next?" Coryn said while trying to swat away some random branches that were flying at her face. She hated the forest, she hated trees, and she hated nature. It was all too green for her liking.

Seth stopped walking and glared at Coryn with mild disdain.

"I mean, what will you do once you've Conjured The Infinite?"

"Power is a means but it isn't an end," Seth sighed. "This process isn't easy otherwise everyone would be able to contact The Infinite. The last time someone successfully communicated with The Infinite was in Ancient Rome and the Roman Empire toppled that same night. The pursuit of ultimate power is dangerous but the rewards are worthwhile. Try to think of tonight as your first date with The Infinite."

Seth, Julee, Coryn, Jack and Lawrence were so deep into the woods that the world was enclosed in an array of twisted topiary. They could barely see the night sky such was the bleak density of the forest. Fortunately they had come prepared with battery operated torches and goody bags crammed with sweets and chocolates and booze.

The alcohol had been Julee's contribution, of course.

Seth suddenly stopped walking and everybody gradually

halted to stand behind him.

"We're here," he said quietly.

An exciting, expectant hush descended upon the group of teenagers. They didn't have long to wait for Seth's instructions.

A lone torch beam illuminated Seth's beautiful face in the darkness. Everything was nearly in place to begin the incantation, but he had to direct the others into their positions, so that they could bear witness to his ascension towards ultimate power.

"Who's got the candles?"

"I have!" Reet lifted up a small Lush tote bag and waved it. The smell of sweet soap lingered in the bag but only Reet could smell it.

"Who has the incense?"

"Right here!" Coryn opened up her jacket to reveal some joss sticks.

"Now I'm warning you," Reet piped up again, "I won't help you complete this ritual if you intend harming any animals. I'm not up for animal sacrifice. Okay?"

Seth cringed but kept a smile on his face. Reet was unbearably predictable.

"Animal sacrifice doesn't serve any practical use in magick any more. We all sacrifice animals whenever we order a Big Mac at McDonald's. It would be a hollow gesture."

This seemed to placate Reet and she stood quietly waiting for Seth's next order.

"Who has the print-out?"

There was no reply. Everybody flashed their torch beams at each other in an attempt to search out the location of a print-out Seth had made earlier in The Cottage.

"Who has the print-out?" Seth yelled irately. He wasn't a particularly patient person, so he tended to shout a lot, his voice always close to the edge of hysteria.

But when Seth spoke again, his voice wasn't hysterical, instead it was heavy with embarrassment. He didn't quite know how to say it, so he just blurted out the truth.

"Oh, I've got the print-out right here."

A short pause followed until,

"Now we can begin..."

Some time passed and the tenants of The Cottage, under the watchful eye of Seth, arranged the candles and the joss sticks into the pattern of a large circle. For the sake of Halloween, Coryn had tried pushing for a pentagram, a suggestion which had been met with enthusiasm by the others, but which was ultimately overruled by Seth.

The ritual, he explained in his dreadfully familiar tone of condescension, required a circle not a pentagram. They weren't doing some bargain basement witchcraft; they were attempting to gain the favour of an entity from a completely unknown realm.

"How will you know if The Infinite hears your message?" Reet asked cautiously. She was starting to wonder what she was actually doing in the middle of a creepy forest on Halloween. Suddenly this didn't seem like such a fun idea to her.

"According to everything I've read on the subject, The Infinite will dispatch three of his Ambassadors down from the higher dimension. They will judge whether or not I'm worthy of their lord's power. Then I'll pop off to see The Infinite and return as a god, at which point I will vapourise you all into dust with a wave of my hand!"

Then he added a hasty but not very convincing, "Just joking."

Jack uttered a nervy little laugh. He sounded like a demented donkey at the fun fair.

"This is freaky stuff, man! I feel like I've smoked a stash of Lawrence's blow."

Seth pointedly ignored the crass outburst and continued speaking:

"According to this print-out, The Infinite will send us a sign, some kind of confirmation, and then…" Seth strained in the dark to see the tatty print-out, "'…the eyes of the sky will open.'"

"What the heck does that mean? It makes no sense." Reet proclaimed.

"I have no idea at all," Seth said with a shrug, "I'm sure it will be spectacular."

Julee aimed her torch beam at the wad of paper in Seth's trembling hands. Her eyes were slowly beginning to acclimatize themselves to the dusky gloom, but she liked waving the torch around, it reminded her of a light show she'd seen in a really cool nightclub a few years ago. She'd printed off a stack of fake IDs that night. Smiling at the memories, Julee suddenly felt a yearning to go on a proper night out again.

"What is that print-out anyway?" Julee asked. "Why is it so important?"

Seth pulled the prints away from the torch beam in a fit of pique. He was beginning to tire of the unrelenting questioning. Not for the first time that night did he wonder whether or not he should have brought these idiots along with him.

"I found a link on Wikipedia and clicked on it. The detail on how to Conjure The Infinite was all there in front of me, so I just printed it off and now I'm going to test it out with you lot. It was really quite helpful actually."

"Wikipedia is very useful," Reet said quietly.

Julee, however, knew a big fat lie when she heard one.

"So let me get this right," Julee said skeptically. "You got a spell to invoke unearthly powers off a website you found on

Wikipedia? I don't believe you. Where did you really get the spell? Who gave it to you?"

Seth's impatient reply echoed across the depressing forest undergrowth. "Even if I'm lying, do you honestly think I'll ever tell you where I actually got the spell from?"

Since everybody in the small group was bombarding Seth for answers, Jack decided to ask the one obvious question nobody else had even thought about asking:

"Where did you get the idea to call The Infinite anyway?"

Seth didn't reply with words, instead he lit a candle, placed it gently onto the ground, and allowed himself to smile grimly at a private joke.

"A friend gave me the idea," was all he would say.

Thunder followed lightning and lightning followed thunder. They waltzed together in the heavens above, twisting and turning in complex motions, pausing every now and then for the benefit of the world below.

"Etinifni eht fo rewop emilbus eht nopu llac I!" Seth called out grandly.

The sound of thunder rumbled in the near distance.

"Litnu, litnu, litnu revo ssorc lliw eciov ym!"

Lightning parted the black clouds beyond the forest and the trees trembled softly.

"Srefsnart rewop eht dna yawa skool esrevinu eht!"

Seth pointed a candle in the direction of Coryn, Reet, Jack, Julee and Lawrence.

None of them had any idea what he'd just shouted, but they hadn't like the sinister tone in his voice as he had cried out into the night.

A new sound was born in the cold darkness. The teenagers

heard it moving toward them, but they couldn't get a fix on where it was coming from, so they all fanned out to find the source of the disturbance.

"Don't break the circle!" Seth suddenly yelled.

"I'm scared!" Reet cried out as the strange noises grew in intensity.

"I'm not!" Coryn lied as she stepped back towards the circle. "This stuff isn't real."

The noise was edging nearer to the little group. It sounded like the beating of wings, a fluttering chorus made up of a thousand flapping feathers encircling the night. The darkness twisted and entwined the entire forest.

"Thgir yb enim si taht rewop eht em evig ho!" Seth chanted with a steady voice.

Reet opened her mouth and screamed fearfully, but her cries were drowned out by a well-timed clap of thunder. The candles flickered and the murkiness in the woods shifted into shapes and concepts that only Seth could see and appreciate. He threw his hands up and screamed at The Infinite to give him complete attention.

"Won etinifni eht fo tfig eht em esufer!"

It didn't take long for The Infinite to respond to Seth's request.

The candles ignited with an astonishing gush of flame. The fire whooshed upwards and illuminated the forest, exploding the bleak night with dazzling bursts of magick. The fiery light also revealed the source of the strange fluttering noises, the cause of the sounds that had terrified everyone within the circle of magick.

There were thousands of shiny black ravens perched on each branch of every tree throughout the forest. They looked down upon the tenants of The Cottage with derisive little eyes. The black birds were now animated by the will of a higher power; a force conjured into reality by Seth Kevorkian. And it was very angry.

The ravens cawed every now and then, a nasty bird-shriek of resentment. They knew the ritual had not been completed and they waited intently to see whether Seth had the tenacity to do what had to be done in order to finish off the spell.

Unfortunately, Seth had absolutely no idea what to do next.

"The spell has gone wrong," he said hoarsely, "this shouldn't be happening!"

"WHAT?" Julee choked on her own fear.

"I haven't performed the ritual correctly," Seth said in a fearful voice.

"If you can perform a ritual, then you can reverse it!" Reet cried out.

They didn't get a chance to find out. Some of the ravens, the flock closest to Seth, flapped their wings and cawed furiously. The candles flickered out and the forest gloom dimmed the artificial light from the torches. The little group was in the middle of the woods on Halloween, trapped and alone, encircled by an army of birds.

"We have to get out of here now…" Reet said.

Coryn's nerve broke first. Far from being as brave as she earlier claimed, she was the most terrified out of everybody. Not only had her resolve been shaken by the alien sounds of the forest, but seeing the ravens freaked Coryn out in a way she hadn't anticipated. She didn't want to remain any longer in the circle created by Seth.

With a whimper of fright, Coryn darted deep into the forest, quickly becoming one with the shadows.

"CORYN!" Lawrence shouted hoarsely. "COME BACK!"

The ravens erupted into a writhing, tangled mass of feather and beak. Even Seth was taken aback by the sheer ferocity of the creatures; he stumbled out of the circle and started running for his life. The ravens attacked without thought, their bodies becoming small missiles, living artillery with grasping talons.

Reet looked up as one of the birds tore down at her, its claws slicing a random pattern onto her face. She screamed with distress and fright, but she couldn't fight off her attacker. It was soon followed by more and more eager birds. They enveloped Reet and she hysterically slapped them away from her face.

The others suffered the consequences of breaking the magick circle.

Jack punched at anything that moved, accidentally striking Lawrence's hairless head at one point. When he got a chance, he bolted past the trees and shrubbery. Lawrence's defence against the attack was to throw his arms into random shapes, but the ravens wouldn't give up the fight. Julee was slightly luckier. Her first reaction was to pick up one of the trick-or-treat bags crammed with food and hurl it chaotically around. This did more damage to the birds than Julee had dared hope.

Suddenly it was all over.

Lawrence, Reet, Jack and Seth stood alone amongst the trees. They were scratched and bleeding, and thankfully still alive.

But where was Coryn?

Coryn didn't stop running until the birds gave up on her. Not exactly the fittest of people, she heaved and sucked in huge gulps of air, trying to slow down the frenzied thumping of her heart. Her body weakly fell onto a tree and she closed her eyes, vainly attempting to block the forest from her sight.

A sound — a slight movement, a snapping of twigs — alerted Coryn to the fact she wasn't alone anymore. She opened her eyes and caught sight of a lonely figure in the distance. The shape was obscured by trees but Coryn could see it watching her intently. It was a person shape, someone lurking in the darkness, waiting for…what?

Coryn jumped up and ran off in the opposite direction and she didn't stop running until her legs gave way and she fell into the soft undergrowth. What if the shape followed her? What if it wanted to kill her? Or do something worse?

Ten minutes passed and Coryn wandered aimlessly through the forest, helpless and pathetic, her low self-esteem and deep feelings of vulnerability finally getting the better of her. She hadn't felt as helpless as this since the day she'd been taken away from her parents. Looking at her surroundings, Coryn realised she couldn't see anything but shadows and trees; the only thing she could do was call for help.

"WHERE ARE YOU?" Coryn screamed at the forest.

WHERE ARE YOU? The forest answered back.

She turned and cupped her hands to her mouth, hoping against all odds that someone might hear her, and follow the sound of her voice.

"ARE YOU THERE?"

ARE YOU THERE? The echo voice said in the distance.

Coryn listened intently but heard nothing. No sound existed amongst the trees.

"CAN YOU HEAR ME?" Coryn yelled at the top of her lungs.

I HEAR YOU…CORYN. Something in the forest chuckled nastily.

Coryn's eyes widened as the echo reached her ears. She instinctively knew that the voice in the forest came from the mouth of someone utterly malevolent. Once more she felt a shockwave of dread brought on by a feeling of complete helplessness. She wished she hadn't run off from the others. She silently vowed never to aid Seth in his stupid magick mumbo jumbo ever again.

A pair of hands grabbed her and pushed her down onto the undergrowth.

"You gross dumb fat cow!" Seth raged at Coryn. "You've ruined everything. I nearly had The Infinite's attention and you ruined it. What are you shouting about?"

Coryn pointed a trembling finger at some trees in the near distance.

"There's someone else in the forest with us!"

"We're the only ones here tonight!" Seth said between gritted teeth.

He was in the grip of a terrible rage, a fury Coryn had rarely seen Seth display openly at The Cottage; he tended to mask his true feelings and motives. But not now. Right now Seth was far more dangerous than any mysterious stranger hiding in the forest. Coryn tried to get up onto her feet, to warn Seth about the shape behind the trees, but Seth kicked her down without mercy.

"Leave me alone!" Coryn cried. "I'll tell Mother you hit me!"

Seth ignored the threat and kicked Coryn again, but this time he put more effort into his attack. His industrial-strength boots knocked the wind out of Coryn and she stumbled heavily against a large oak tree. She tried to escape but Seth caught her easily; he wrapped his hand tightly around Coryn's greasy hair, tugging it until she screamed. Then Seth swung Coryn around and sent her on a rapid journey head first into the large oak. She struck it forcefully and the world buckled around her.

When Coryn woke up from her daze, it wasn't Seth's arms wrapped around her but those of Julee. For once in her life Coryn didn't grumble. She could see Julee was absolutely terrified as well. A strange kind of calmness asserted itself in Coryn despite the peculiar set of circumstances. She looked over at Seth who was innocently explaining that Coryn had been attacked by a mysterious assailant in the woods. The others gasped in awe as Seth explained how he'd probably saved Coryn's life from someone else in the forest; but who was the mysterious person?

"I can't see anyone else out there," Jack said after quickly examining the direction Coryn had pointed towards. His lack of interest in the subject seemed to run contrary to Coryn's assertions that she'd seen someone watching them perform the ritual. But Coryn knew better. Someone else was out there watching them. Someone who had fled deeper into the darkness when Seth arrived and assaulted her.

"I tell you I heard a voice," Coryn said huffily, but she was soundly ignored.

The little group didn't remain in the forest much longer. During the long journey back home to The Cottage, they made a pact not to mention the events of that night ever again. It was too strange and too frightening to relive and much easier to pretend none of it happened.

But Seth didn't forget, not even for a second. It was all he thought about every second of every minute of every hour of the day. He was never quite the same again. He became more determined than ever before to complete the spell as a result of that night in the forest

Perhaps it was the alluring promise of power that fuelled his desperation. Or maybe it was the searing memory of his failure that spurred him onwards.

Whatever the reason behind his newfound resolve, it wasn't long before Seth made another attempt at calling The Infinite — only this time he would succeed…

THE TOTALLY WIRED VEGETARIAN
After The Funeral

"He was completely fixated with The Infinite," Lawrence said weakly. It sounded as though he didn't want to think about The Infinite let alone discuss it aloud.

Lily didn't know exactly what had happened, because the housemates had fallen uncharacteristically silent during dinner, so she attempted to put into words what she'd gleaned from the scraps she'd been fed during their uneasy discussion.

"So you all followed Seth into the forest to cast a magick spell." Lily tried to hide amusement from her voice. "Then what happened?"

"Nothing!" Reet responded swiftly, but Lily instinctively knew there was more to the situation than anyone was fully prepared to admit.

"I know something happened, you just don't want to talk about it."

"You're right," Reet said dismissively, "I *don't* want to talk about it."

Lily boldly switched tactic. She decided the best way to proceed was with courtesy.

"Are you okay?" Lily asked Reet politely.

"Yes," she replied whilst pretending to find her empty plate eternally fascinating.

Courtesy be damned, Lily lashed out and instantly regretted her pettiness:

"Are you up to date with your medication?"

"YES!" Reet shouted, aggravated she'd drawn so much attention to herself.

The digital screaming of emergency alarms filled the entire house before Lily had a chance to argue back.

Mother hit the panic button twice just in case the first strike didn't take effect. Patricia was now completely out of control; Mother could only watch helplessly as her patient hurled two care workers across the room with obscene effortlessness.

"Sausages!" Patricia growled in her deep, masculine voice. "Sausages!"

Mother hastily turned and fled Patricia's velvet cage, pushing herself along the upstairs hall. Not a spry woman by any means, Mother found herself struggling to reach the staircase in time to avoid Patricia's determined pursuit. She was in luck; the alarms had the desired effect: Lily was charging up the long spiral stairs, backed by a team of burly care workers. They looked like a miniature anti-riot squad.

"She's leaving The Cottage tomorrow!" Mother gasped as she caught her breath.

Lily was the personification of serenity as the Abomination shrieked in the background. Her shrieks of fury sounded utterly demonic.

"What set her off this time?" Lily asked with a raise of her eyebrow.

"I don't have a clue, but this is like nothing I've ever seen in all my years…"

"SAUSAGES!" A voice bellowed from the far end of the hallway.

Something suddenly occurred to Lily. It seemed like such an obvious thing to ask:

"When was Patricia last fed?"

Mother looked over at the two care workers behind her, the same two who had suffered the full impact of Patricia's rage. The guilty expressions on their faces only served to confirm the suspicions unfolding in Lily's mind. Mother's self-control was being severely tested by this event; her temper bubbled perilously close to the surface.

"Idiots! You forgot to feed her! Get down to the kitchen and make her…"

"SAUSAGES!" a voice roared from nearby.

"Get her some food before she tears the place apart!" Mother yelled at the quivering yet obedient members of staff.

Julee felt her insides twisting and heaving as the violent racket upstairs increased. But it was a casual declaration from Jack that pushed the post-dinner conversation towards the subject of The Abomination.

"They're only making the problem worse by keeping her locked away."

Everybody at the table turned their collective gaze on Jack and he held his hands up in mock surrender. Coryn's round face betrayed her feelings, she felt herself giving Jack an involuntary smile, but quickly stopped when he looked over at her.

Does he know how much I like him? Coryn thought to herself. *How much did Seth tell him about me?*

"Seth told me the whole story," Jack said smugly.

A thought made of bright red flashed through Coryn's head. She wondered whether Jack had somehow read her mind, but she was relieved to discover he was talking about The Abomination. Coryn breathed out a deep sigh of relief.

"Patricia is prescribed anti-psychosis medication that helps control the worst of her mood swings, right, but the pills have a weird side effect."

Everybody at the table was enraptured by the unexpected gossip. Unaccustomed to being the main character in anyone's story, Jack thrived on the rare sensation of being centre of attention, even if for a few minutes. He dispatched his gossip with an intimate voice in the manner of someone telling a ghost story beside a campfire.

"Patricia's medication also bulks up her weight, that's why she's huge but that's not all, her meds also increase her strength. She's like The Incredible Hulk."

Reet was the first housemate to respond to Jack's tittle-tattle. She uttered an unsympathetic cackle, a noise which surprised Lawrence, because it sounded very unlike her. There was something different about Reet tonight, Lawrence knew this intuitively, but he couldn't quite work out what. Lily could see it as well. Lawrence had spotted Lily scrutinizing Reet with her psychologist expression throughout dinner. He decided to do the same as Lily and watch Reet from a discreet distance.

(This wouldn't be a difficult duty for Lawrence, because he watched Reet every day.)

"She's like The Incredible Hulk? The Abominable Bulk is more like it! Patricia should have been drowned at birth," Reet said between random outbursts of nasty laughter, "she's weak and insignificant. She really *is* an abomination."

Then Reet realised Lawrence was looking at her deeply.

"What the hell are you staring at, baldy?"

The attention of everyone at the table shifted right onto Reet once again. Even Julee was appalled by the uncharacteristic malice she was witnessing from her friend.

"Sorry," Reet said contritely, "I don't know what came over me."

"You're probably stressed by Seth's funeral," Lawrence suggested in a hurt voice.

"Yes," Reet agreed a little too quickly, "I'm stressed by Seth's funeral."

"I don't believe that stuff about Patricia's medication," Julee said thoughtfully, "it sounds like another nasty little rumour invented by Seth."

But the shockwaves generated by Reet's outburst were still being felt at the table; Julee's levelheaded observation was ignored as a result. Nobody spoke for a few minutes until Coryn finally piped up with an observation of her own. As a result of living with each other, everybody in The Cottage knew each other's problems, desires and passions. So Coryn knew exactly how to deliver maximum upset for Reet.

She simply asked her a question.

Yet it was a question everybody in the room wanted Reet to answer, the response to which might help explain her rather odd behaviour throughout dinner. The question mentioned one particular name, a name everybody whispered behind Reet's back…everybody except Seth, of course. He used to unashamedly hurl the forbidden name right at Reet, much to Lily's genuine displeasure. It never happened in the vicinity of Mother, oddly enough. No, Seth was far too clever to be caught out.

What was Coryn's question?

"Have you seen Lloyd recently?" She asked with faux

sweetness.

Reet shot Coryn a look of pure loathing, another uncharacteristic act observed by Lawrence from the comfort of his chair.

Then she replied: "No."

But Reet was lying.

LLOYD, I'M READY TO BE HEARTBROKEN

Whenever Reet felt depressed, she found that a visit to the duck pond at the local park had a remarkably soothing effect on her nerves. In the weeks leading up to Seth's murder, she found herself going to the pond more and more. It soon became her favourite place in the world. It was so peaceful and the animals looked so happy.

Reet had always preferred animals to people. In her experience, people were unpleasant and unreliable. Human beings wrecked the world and filled it with cars, pollution, war, and misery. Animals were beyond all of that. They had no concept of depression, prescription drugs and all the other problems Reet had experienced in her life. The animals just lived a simple life without any guilt or shame.

One day while watching the ducks swimming gently in the water, Reet wished above all else that her life could be as uncomplicated as theirs.

It was during one of her low periods that Reet met Lloyd. He was dark-skinned and beautiful, his hair short and choppy, his left ear adorned by a little diamond stud. Lloyd liked watching the ducks too. In fact Lloyd loved all animals and, unlike Reet, he had the courage of his convictions and did something to help them. Lloyd protected the vulnerable by any means necessary and he wanted Reet to join him in his quest.

"There's a place," Lloyd told Reet during one of their meetings at the duck pond, "a place where animals suffer and men make money from their meat."

"What do they do to them?" Reet asked with a tremor in her question.

"Terrible things," Lloyd said in a soft voice. A gleam filled his eyes, a gleam that might have been excitement — or something else, something much darker.

Plans were made for Reet to meet Lloyd and his gang for the late night mission. Both the date and the time were fixed and Reet promised she would be there no matter what. Lloyd asked only one thing of Reet, and that was for her to bring a friend. For his plan to work, Lloyd required as many people as possible sympathetic to the cause, and though Reet considered Lawrence, she finally settled on Seth.

She wasn't especially keen on Seth being there, but at the time it made good sense: Seth had expressed an interest in animal welfare in the distant past, but also Reet had only just made up with Seth after a particularly vicious quarrel. She thought it would be a nice gesture to invite Seth, to show him there were no hard feelings between them anymore. It was her way of making amends after what happened.

"I'll bring Seth," Reet told Lloyd. "Don't do anything until we get there."

The incident that had sparked the quarrel between Reet and Seth had happened only a few days before the fateful meeting at the duck pond. Reet had stumbled on Seth breaking into Lily's office. She liked Lily enough not to want her private things pinched, so Reet told Seth to stop being a crook. Seth was deaf to her; he was intent on finding something specific that Lily had hidden away, and he wasn't happy about being caught red handed.

"What are you after anyway?" Reet demanded.

"Lily has something I need," Seth replied acidly, "I must have it."

"Then go and ask her for it. Don't break into her office like a scumbag."

Seth swore at Reet and she swore back at him. Then Seth spat on Reet's face and a violent confrontation broke out. The argument was so ferocious that it roused everyone in The Cottage out of their sleep. And who happened to be first on the scene but Lily herself! Flustered and carrying a little red diary and pen, she arrived promptly as a result of enduring a late shift. Her eyes expressed naked horror when she realised Seth had been rifling through her personal things.

Seth loudly promised Reet that she would suffer for her interference, but in the end nothing came of it and he apologised to her for the fuss the next morning.

Despite Lloyd's request that everybody should dress in black, Seth decided to turn up at the meeting point looking like a human traffic light. He was clad in what looked suspiciously like a green fur jacket so bright it seemed to glow in the dark. It was the kind of jacket that wouldn't look out of place at a rave, but looked totally incompatible with any other situation.

He quickly assured Reet and the others that his horrid green jacket wasn't fashioned from real fur, but nobody believed his denials and his choice of clothing went down like a cup of mouldy milk with the vegans. Despite her mortification with Seth's behaviour, Reet remained. She knew how quick-witted Seth was and she didn't want to be verbally mangled in front of her new friends.

The little group of animal activists, however, didn't know anything about Seth other than the fact he was an outsider wearing a distasteful jacket. Their mutual anger quickly increased until Lloyd stepped in to prevent a lynching.

Lloyd's voice, when he used it properly, held weight. It was the voice of a born leader, a voice Reet would follow to the ends of the universe and back.

"Nobody touches him!" Lloyd yelled. "He's here with my friend."

Then Lloyd looked at Reet and smiled warmly. He nodded smoothly at Seth.

"Do you trust him?" Lloyd asked Reet.

Strong feelings of uneasiness suddenly absorbed Reet. She felt a great sense of uncertainty about Seth, but this passed and she found herself sticking up for her housemate. They might never be the best of friends, but they were both from The Cottage, and that alone was enough to inspire a sense of loyalty in her.

"Yes. I trust Seth. We're tight."

"I trust you too, Reeta," Seth said, but his face was vacant.

Lloyd seemed satisfied with Reet's endorsement. "Good. Everybody follow me!"

Without any further words, the little group headed off into the night.

Two minutes passed before the little white van came into view.

The inside of the van was extremely dirty. There was an old carpet on the floor of the vehicle, but it was thick with filth and grime. The stench of decaying egg and cucumber sandwiches filled the van's innards, an aroma not suited to everyone.

"This is totally disgusting," Seth said despairingly.

"Shut up!" a voice from one of the protesters snapped at him. They still hadn't forgiven him for his fur jacket faux pas. If this bothered Seth, he certainly didn't show it. He was perched next to Reet, trying not to sit on the dirty carpet. He failed however and every now and then, on route to their destination, the van would run over some bumps and Seth would tumble onto Reet and Lloyd.

"When will we get there?" Reet asked Lloyd.

"Eventually," his voice came out the dimness.

The van eventually stopped close to an old factory.

Reet's initial reaction to the old factory was that of extreme dislike. It was an old building with two large windows that looked like big evil eyes, and it was bathed in a harsh blue neon light which flickered intermittently. The area around the place was full of industrial sounds and a smell that made her want to heave up her insides.

Goose pimples raised on Reet's arms and neck.

"My skin is crawling," Reet said as she ran a hand through her spiky elfin hair.

"Where are we?" Seth asked Lloyd.

"It's a meat-packing factory called The Steak Place. Animals go in through that entrance — that one over there — and they come out as pies. One of my people got video footage of cows being tortured by the slaughtermen and their filthy knives. This place reeks of death. We must rescue our animal friends."

Seth coughed a laugh and quickly covered his mouth to muffle the sound.

Lloyd shook his head in frustration. He was finally beginning to lose patience with Seth Kevorkian. His arrogant tone of voice was unceasingly disrespectful and Lloyd couldn't be bothered with people who mocked his opinions.

"Do you ever take anything seriously?"

"I'm here," Seth retorted. "I want to help as much as you do."

"What now?" Reet said, skillfully averting another argument.

The little mass of animal activists crowded around Lloyd and waited for instructions. It was clear they had done this in the past. They were a unit and would do anything Lloyd wanted in order to save animals.

"We head in through the back door over there." Lloyd pointed at a small emergency exit door located at the side of the building. "It's been left open by a janitor sympathetic to our plight."

Nobody noticed Seth attempting to stifle more laughter. Nobody, that is, except Reet. That was when she knew bringing Seth on this mission was a mistake, but it was too late to turn back. She glared angrily at Seth who had now resorted to masking his laughter with a clenched fist.

Lloyd outlined the rest of the plan while zipping his black hoodie.

"We get inside, find the livestock, then we unlock the door and release them all. Its night shift and we can get them outside under cover of darkness. Remember to wear your masks, because there's CCTV inside, and under no circumstances can we be seen. The building is fitted with a panic button. Once pressed will send a signal to the police station. Their reaction speed is very fast. If that button gets pressed, the police will get here in five minutes."

Reet felt a keen edginess cut through her, but it felt good, and she realised at that moment that she was going to do something good for the animals and for herself.

The endless depression which gripped her relaxed itself for the first time in years.

If the outside of the factory smelled horrible, the inside was infinitely worse, and Reet had to steady herself against Lloyd to prevent the contents of her breakfast coming up. In truth she liked the feeling of her body pressed against his, and she knew he liked it too, but the moment passed like most things in life.

"Where are the animals being kept?" Seth stepped into the middle of the hallway and looked around with a keen interest. The sight of her garish housemate moving around the corridors in a green fur jacket broke Reet out of her romantic reveries. It was time for war, not love. Even now Reet thought she could hear the sounds of the awful drills and cleavers and conveyor belts and animals. She was going to save them and, in a strange sort of way, save herself. She needed to see this through to the end.

"The animals have to be around here somewhere," Reet said firmly.

One of the protesters, an acne ridden teenage boy with ginger hair, produced a crumpled tatty piece of paper from his pocket.

"We walk down this corridor and head towards the first turning on the left. That'll lead us to the holding den."

"Let's go and save the cows!" Seth shouted theatrically.

"Shut up!" Lloyd hissed at him as they all headed down the corridors. "Are you trying to get us caught? There might not be many people in the factory tonight, but there are still people, and it only takes one of them to hit the panic button."

Reet could only hear the sound of her heart and the regular stomp of her Dr Martens as they pounded the floor. She turned into the first corridor on the left and advanced towards what she hoped would be the detention area. She could hear soft mooing from scared cows and her heart overflowed with compassion.

"This is it!" Lloyd cried out, his voice alight with tension.

Lloyd hit a switch and the detention room doors opened to reveal the world outside. The cows didn't need to be persuaded to stay, so they departed quickly, helped along by the little gang of activists. It was all over in five minutes.

Reet watched the animals walk towards freedom: beautiful, wonderful freedom.

Then someone hit the panic button.

Reet, Lloyd and the others turned to flee out of the emergency exit only to find heavy metal shutters had suddenly dropped down. There was no escape that way for any of them. Reet whirled around and headed towards the door she'd entered from, hoping to make it up through the harshly lit corridors before anybody could check the detention room. She would have made it but something happened to stop her.

There was a blur of bright green followed by a stained smile. Then the only available escape exit slammed and locked. The activists yelled in fear and confusion.

With both entrances inaccessible, the room was now their prison.

"Seth!" Reet screamed in terror. "What are you doing?"

"I'm leaving you to be caught."

"Why are you doing this?" Lloyd shouted. "The animals aren't safe yet. They could still be rounded up! Let us go or the police will catch us."

"I don't care about animals, I don't care about anything except myself," said the voice from behind the door. Reet realised to her dismay that Seth was completely sincere; Seth really didn't care about anyone other than Seth.

"I *want* you to get caught." Seth's voice was dreamy. "I'm leaving you here."

The familiar crushing weight of depression slammed down on Reet as the enormity of her predicament became obvious. *This is bad*, she thought, *this is really bad*.

"Please open the door!" Reet yelled. "Mother will throw me out of The Cottage, and I'll have nowhere else to go. My parents are in jail and I've got no family."

"Good!" Seth snarled. "I hope you suffer."

"Why are you doing this?" Reet's voice was flat, lifeless. Her depression was in control and she couldn't fight it away.

"You're a hypocritical bitch," Seth's tone was triumphant, "you grassed on me when I broke into Lily's office and then you break into this place to impress some vegans!"

One or two of the activists trapped in the room gasped at the hate in Seth's words. Even Lloyd was surprised at the masterful elegance of Seth's treachery. But nobody could do anything other than listen as Seth continued his unpleasant gloating.

"All you idiots need to go out and get proper jobs!"

Police sirens echoed in the distance. They were getting closer.

"I've got to go now," Seth trilled delightedly. "I'm going to head back home and have a nice steak pie for dinner. Oh and my jacket *is* made from real fur."

Reet slid down the door, crying for Seth to let her out, but he delivered one last stinging riposte before leaving them to their fate:

"You should have minded your own business, Reet. Goodbye forever!"

"I'll kill you for this!" Lloyd roared over the noise of sirens.

Seth didn't hear his threat, because he was long gone.

The police were very thorough upon their appearance outside The Steak Place. Arriving in a blaze of noise and sirens and flashing lights, their first act was to search the battered old white van used by the activists to move from factory to factory.

When they did, they found a quantity of illegal drugs stuffed underneath a dirty rug on the van's floor. The drugs had been placed there by Seth earlier that night; his final, devastating reprisal against Reet.

Not that the police believed Reet's denials. Why should they? Reet lived in The Cottage, a place full of troubled youths, so it made perfect sense to them that she would probably take drugs. All the police knew for certain was that someone had hit the panic button and locked the criminals in a room used to keep the livestock.

They were grateful for the help; it kept things neat and tidy for their reports.

Reet and Lloyd were cuffed and bundled into a waiting patrol car. The arresting officer was a rotund man in an ill-fitting uniform called Sgt. McAllister. He glowered at Reet with the expression as a man who had just soiled his shoes with something nasty. Reet didn't speak on route to the station, she didn't utter a sound. She couldn't form words to express her terror.

But Lloyd was different. He smoldered with dangerous intensity. Even though his teeth were gritted together, Reet could clearly hear him muttering under his breath:

"Kill him. I'm going to kill him. I'm going to kill Seth Kevorkian."

A startling coincidence happened only a few days after Reet was caught breaking into The Steak Place. Sgt. McAllister, he of the stern voice and tight cuffs, was dispatched to look into a mysterious phone message placed by an anonymous caller.

According to the phone call, there was a dead body abandoned up on the cliffs.

Sgt. McAllister only discovered Seth's corpse as a result of this tip-off.

When Reet finally heard the news of Seth's murder, she wondered whether or not Lloyd had actually carried out his threat. But she didn't dare say anything; she was scared Lloyd would return and finish off what he might have started with Seth.

UNDERCOVER KEPT
After The Funeral

Dessert was cancelled and the disappointed housemates decided to abandon the dining room in favour of fun and games elsewhere in The Cottage. But heading upstairs to their rooms wasn't an option because of the ongoing situation with The Abomination. The little group split as a result and Julee found herself sitting in the conservatory with windows wide open. Between her fingers was a cigarette butt, casually smoked into nonexistence, but essential because Julee's body was craving a nicotine fix. Smoking was her new addiction now she'd given up alcohol.

Julee sat there in blissful silence, pondering the events of the day, wondering whether or not she'd be able to leave The Cottage any time soon. It wasn't that Julee hated living there; she enjoyed it, because she'd never known such stability, but she wanted freedom from Mother and the other housemates.

"Julee," a voice gasped behind her, thick with phony concern. "Are you smoking?"

This, Julee thought sadly, *is exactly why I want to leave The Cottage.*

She would have thrown the incriminating cigarette away on any normal day, but she was so fatigued that she couldn't be bothered getting rid of the evidence. She allowed Coryn to stalk into the conservatory and have her little moment of triumph.

"Does Mother know about your smoking habit?" Coryn asked in a snide voice.

Julee insolently blew a cloud of smoke right into Coryn's face.

"You know fine well she doesn't. If you're going to stick me in, just do it."

Coryn wavered by the door, deciding whether or not to call Julee's bluff, but she decided against it. As much as Julee annoyed her, Coryn knew it would be foolish to antagonise her too much. Coryn didn't want the formidable Julee as an enemy.

"Sit down, Coryn." Julee motioned towards a white plastic chair opposite her.

Coryn might not have wanted Julee as an enemy, but she certainly didn't want her as a friend either. She thought about refusing Julee's request, but she soon realised that she couldn't decline the invitation. There was something troubled in Julee's expression; this intrigued Coryn, because she knew it took a lot to bother Julee.

"What is it?" Coryn said, trying to get comfortable on the little plastic chair.

"This probably won't surprise you, but I'm thinking about Seth."

"We're all thinking about Seth. Even Reet is acting weirdly. It's this memorial dinner. Why do we have to go? I'm not even hungry! I've been eating all day long."

"I'm sure you have," Julee said.

Coryn suddenly felt self-conscious about her weight.

("Why can't you get a boyfriend?" Seth's voice echoed in her memory. "Why can't you be more like Julee?")

Anger flared up from deep inside Coryn. "Are you insulting me?"

"Don't be stupid. You know I'm not a nasty bitch."

Julee took one last puff of her gnarled cigarette butt and flicked it out the nearby window. Then she turned and dropped a bombshell:

"I think Seth was murdered by someone here at The Cottage."

Astonishment slackened Coryn's jaw.

"Why do you think that? You must have a reason!"

"I can't tell you," Julee said quietly, "you wouldn't believe me."

"Gut instinct?" Coryn asked suspiciously.

"No…something happened. I said you wouldn't believe me, I mean it."

Coryn's voice raised a pitch. "Am I a suspect?"

"It might be any one of us," Julee snapped impatiently. The conversation wasn't going the way she'd expected. "We all have reasons and we all hated his guts."

"I didn't hate Seth," Coryn cried out.

"After what he did to you, darling, you probably hated him the most."

Coryn didn't have time to defend or guard herself against Julee's accusations; Lily suddenly joined the girls in the conservatory, her presence endeing their discussion. Despite looking slightly flushed due to her struggle with The Abomination, she wore a wide smile upon her face as she addressed the two girls.

"The situation is officially over! You can head to your rooms if you like."

Something faintly offensive to Lily's nose caused her to recoil in disgust.

"Has someone been smoking in here?"

Coryn locked herself in her bedroom at the first possible opportunity. Julee's words had freaked her out beyond reason, not because the idea of one of her housemates being a killer seemed unlikely, but because it seemed very likely indeed.

She threw herself down onto her bed and replayed the conversation back and forward in her head, editing it down to the important bits:

("I think Seth was murdered by someone at The Cottage."

"Why do you think that? You must have a reason!"

"I can't tell you. You wouldn't believe me.")

Coryn sighed. It sounded like a sonic boom in her bedroom.

"How much do you know, Julee? And how the hell did you find out?"

ALWAYS LISTEN TO
YOUR SOCIAL WORKER

Julee's first social worker, a ghastly little man called Mr. Mannerly, had always warned her about the dangers of leaving her drinks unattended in night clubs. But she didn't pay the slightest bit of attention to Mr. Mannerly. His name might as well have been Mr. Misery, because he was forever moaning about the world. Targets included the evils of drinking, the insidious dangers of STDs, the knife crime gangs patrolling the streets, and the psychological murder committed by hip-hop music. Julee chose to ignore Mr. Mannerly's moans because she wasn't a whore, didn't associate with knife gangs, hated hip-hop, and genuinely assumed nobody would dare spike her drink. That sort of thing only happened to fools who didn't finish their glasses in one gulp!

Julee felt she was many things, but she didn't consider herself to be a fool.

In hindsight, that was a rather stupid assertion on her part.

However — and this is very important — the following chain of events came about *because* someone spiked her drink. The night Julee's drink was spiked with an unknown substance was the same night she met the ghost of Seth Kevorkian...

Julee had always been a bit of a party animal. She had learned this behaviour from her parents who loved nothing more than opening their house up to everybody in the street. Their parties were legendary for a) the volume of free booze and b) the fact they would last for days on end and c) Julee always being the last girl standing.

Julee was an alcoholic by the time she was nine and became sober on her fourteenth birthday. When she turned fifteen, the social workers came and took her away to The Cottage. It didn't matter where Julee lived though, because Julee lived to party.

Three days after Seth Kevorkian's corpse had been discovered atop the burning cliffs, Julee decided to go clubbing, if only to cheer herself up. There was a new nightspot opening down in The Village — or rather the previous nightclub had rebranded for the umpteenth time for tax evasion purposes — and Julee wanted to try out the newly christened 'Tronic'. Julee loved the new name, it sounded mysterious and cool. The only problem in getting to the Tronic was an exasperating curfew Mother imposed on all the residents of The Cottage.

Curfews, Mother informed her, instilled discipline. Julee felt like screaming.

It was Reet who inadvertently gave her an idea of how to get around Mother's fun-killing curfew. They'd been at the dining room table in their pyjamas, snacking on dried fruit and nuts, when Julee confessed her frustrations about the Cottage curfew.

"You could just...I don't know...sneak out the window after dark?" Reet said.

Julee gave Reet a high five before going back to her dried fruit.

"What a great idea. It's obvious and simple, we should do it!"

"We should?" Reet gulped.

"Yes! Let's live a little. Being cooped up in this place is depressing me, which is saying a lot Reet, because there are probably antidepressants in the tap water. But I need to get out of here for a while, and so do you."

Reet looked slightly nervous at the idea of sneaking out with Julee. She had recently been caught breaking into a slaughterhouse with some animal rights activists and had nearly ended up in prison for her role in the incident. Reet reminded Julee about this, but if she thought it would discourage her, she was completely misguided.

Julee wanted Reet as a clubbing partner whether she liked it or not.

Reet continued trying to resist Julee's encouraging comments.

"It seems really crass to go out clubbing so soon after Seth's… death."

She didn't want to say the word 'murder' out loud.

"Seth doesn't care if we go out. He's dead and gone!" Julee cooed seductively.

"He might be dead," Reet mumbled nervously, "I wouldn't say he's gone."

Reet's comment sounded a tad melodramatic to Julee's ears. She would, of course, come to reassess this opinion only a couple of hours later, but right now her only priority was to get into The Tronic. She could feel Reet's resolve failing.

"We'll never have to suffer Seth's bitchy brilliance ever again. Let's have a night out before we both go crazy."

Reet giggled at Julee's inelegant choice of words.

"You could ask Jack, he'd go with you to Tronic. He'd go anywhere with you."

"Jack? No way! I want it to be just us girls. Come on!"

It didn't take long for Reet to change her mind. She did this a lot. The two friends made secret plans to sneak out of their bedroom windows and return to their rooms at a reasonable hour. Nobody would know they'd gone.

"Nuts?" Reet asked Julee, gently pushing the bowl of dried fruit towards her.

"Just as God made me," Julee laughed.

"Welcome to my life," Reet replied quietly. She didn't seem quite as jolly as Julee, but she smiled nonetheless. Then they ate the rest of their breakfast in peace.

Fuelled by a nice breakfast and bonded by the conspiracy brewing between them, Julee and Reet wandered into The Village market to buy some clothes for their secret night out. Julee couldn't believe the difference in Reet after just a few hours in her company, she was a totally different girl to the familiar pixie-haired depressive. There was a real glow of jubilation radiating from deep within Reet and all because of Julee.

The only dark spot came when Julee asked a question she shouldn't have asked:

"What actually happened at the meat packing factory?"

Reet gave a terse one word reply. But Julee flinched as soon as Reet spoke it aloud.

"Seth…"

On the way back to The Cottage, the two girls decided to stop off at the local psychic parlour for a quick consultation. Julee had never taken such things seriously, but she got an allowance as a resident in The Cottage, and decided to spend her money unwisely. Reet, on the other hand, was excited to know the future. On seeing Reet's delight at the prospect of having her fortune told, Julee pretended to be just as enthusiastic when she walked through the doors of the tiny shop.

The window advertised with the words:

CAMPBELL DEVINE'S PSYCHIC EMPIRE!
He Is Psychic And You Are Not!

Campbell himself, sadly, looked preposterous in his ludicrous outfit. He appeared ostentatiously from behind a set of tinseled curtains wearing a silver foil suit and sparkly purple tie. His clothing made him look like a deranged ice lolly.

It took Julee's full self-control not to laugh in front of the fresh-faced psychic.

"Sit down," he said in a dreamy Irish voice, "sit down and let the power of your aura reach me. I can see tomorrow and the next day, for I am psychic."

"This guy is a fraud and a waste of money," Julee whispered at Reet.

"Do you want me to go first?" Reet whispered back.

"Go ahead!"

Campbell motioned for Reet to take a seat in front of him. Julee watched with interest as he started performing his 'psychic warm up' rituals which involved him closing his eyes, waving his fingers, chanting gibberish and looking over at his laptop.

(Julee didn't quite get why he had a laptop sitting beside him.)

Campbell Devine's eyes suddenly snapped open. They were wide with fright, not just mild anxiety, but proper visible horror from sights only his eyes could fathom.

"You both live in The Cottage."

It wasn't a question, more like an accusation.

"Yes," Reet answered politely.

"You both knew Seth Kevorkian."

Again, it sounded like an accusation to Julee, rather than a question.

"He passed away a few days ago," Reet replied helpfully.

Julee nearly laughed again at Reet's use of the phrase 'passed away', which was a sweet but grossly inaccurate description of what had happened to Seth. The words 'passed away' made it sound like Seth had died a peaceful death, but his death had been far from peaceful; someone had deliberately aimed a gun at his chest and pulled a trigger.

"She shot him," Campbell babbled, "He shot him."

Julee noticed that Campbell's strange accent had by now completely disappeared, replaced by a posh intonation, but she didn't mention this because the psychic seemed close to taking a nervous breakdown. He kept repeating words, chanting them over and over again, and it was beginning to frighten Reet.

"I can see him," Campbell gasped, "he actually managed it."

"What are you talking about?" Julee snapped irritably.

"What did Seth do?" Reet asked fearfully. But she knew exactly what he meant.

"He contacted The Infinite," Campbell said quietly, "I told him not to do that."

Julee and Reet both looked at each other with expressions of shock mixed with astonishment. The accuracy behind Campbell's prediction freaked the two girls out.

"The Infinite has heard his call and granted his request. The Ambassadors have been dispatched from the higher dimensions to complete the deal. They are close, so very close. They dance in darkness. Soon we will bear witness to their power. They want Seth more than anything. He is still here with us!"

"I don't understand any of this," Reet said in a tiny voice.

Julee had heard enough. She decided the time was right to intervene.

"We're getting out of here!" Julee snapped at Campbell.

"Mr. Mannerly is right," Campbell cried out, "remember and cover your drink!"

"I'll cover you in bruises if you don't shut your mouth!"

Campbell looked at Reet. An implication unknown to Julee blazed from his eyes.

"His voice is in your ear."

The two girls stumbled outside and ran back to The Cottage without saying a single word.

Later that same night, once the two girls had calmed down, they got their clothes ready for the club and waited patiently for the lights to go out. The main door was locked but Julee had already planned for this; earlier that day she'd pinched a ladder from the greenhouse and propped it up beneath Reet's window.

"I thought the lights would never go out," Julee whispered as she climbed down the rungs. The night air was cold but bracing. Reet was slightly conscious of the skirt she was wearing and was grateful to go out of the window first. At one point she nearly gave the game away when she spotted a spider crawling across the pane. Reet had a morbid fear of spiders, the sight of which unnerved her, but Julee covered Reet's mouth before she could scream and wake everybody up.

The two girls then put on their heels and crept away from The Cottage, trying to smother giggles and any other noise, but not quite succeeding.

When they finally arrived at the new nightclub, it came as something of a relief to see lots of other clubbers sampling the nightlife.

"I think we're the youngest people here," Reet said nervously.

"But your ID says otherwise," Julee said mischievously.

Reet gasped as Julee fished two fake ID cards out of her bag and waved them happily. Reet suddenly felt much better as she came to the conclusion that she might finally enjoy herself. Campbell Devine's words had upset her earlier, but his dire warnings felt like a lifetime ago, and Reet was desperate to let her short hair down.

The noise level in the club was immense and glasses on the tables vibrated under the sonic offensive of the innovative new sound system. Julee couldn't hear a word coming out of Reet's mouth, so she randomly nodded every now and then, in between sips of her cocktail. Julee didn't actually want to drink too much. She kept telling herself she was in control of her drink intake. It wasn't in control of her. She had to remember that she could resist her own self-indulgence.

It was four empty cocktail glasses later before Julee noticed someone near the bar, a man with greasy hair and small piggy eyes, looking over at her intently.

What a creep! Julee thought rebelliously. *He keeps staring at me, as though he's waiting for something to happen.*

She looked up at Reet whose lips moved quickly but made no sense whatsoever.

The music seemed to get louder until the beat of the bass vibrated deafeningly inside her skull. Julee closed her eyes and sipped her drink until it was finished. How many drinks had she finished off? And why did that last one taste so bitter?

Julee opened her eyes and found the nightclub was empty

and silent. The lights suddenly turned from ambient to harsh green neon, illuminating the guts of The Tronic with an eerie green wash. She could feel the heat of the spotlights on her skin, which now crawled with anxious anticipation.

Suddenly Julee became aware that she was no longer alone in the club.

"Reet!" Julee called out. "Where are you?"

"I'm standing right behind you," Reet's voice said joyously.

But it wasn't Reet standing behind Julee. It was Seth Kevorkian.

"Hello," said a murky voice, "I've been waiting for you."

He walked into view, his footsteps shattering the silence, but his form cast no shadow on any walls. Wrapped around him was a crimson robe, the kind of garment only a self-assured warlock could wear with confidence, because anybody else wearing it would look utterly comical. Not even Campbell Devine could wear that robe without appearing even sillier than usual.

Julee had a peculiar feeling she was no longer in The Tronic.

"Where are we?" Julee asked.

"We're in limbo," Seth grinned evilly.

Julee looked around but she could only see the empty nightclub.

"What's it like?" Julee asked her old housemate. "Being dead, I mean."

Seth took a few minutes to think of a fitting response that would best encapsulate the forbidding and unknowable experience of death.

"Being dead," Seth said eventually, "is a bit like...living in Bournemouth."

"Bournemouth?" Julee's voice strained with incredulity. She

had never been to Bournemouth. Her family didn't do holidays.

"It makes perfect sense if you know the full story."

"Bournemouth?" Julee repeated. She didn't quite understand Seth's reasoning.

"I went to Bournemouth years ago as a kid. My dad sent me there to live with my gran. He said he saw nothing of himself in me. It didn't matter anyway. I wanted to see somewhere new and extraordinary, a place full of magick and miracles. Bournemouth held so many possibilities...until I actually got there. It was hell, Julee. I'm being serious. Bournemouth is Hell."

"Talking about the land of the dead," Julee said bluntly, "you're already there."

"Nearly but not quite," Seth replied in a deceptively soft voice.

"So why are we having this friendly chat? You've spoke more to me in the last few minutes than you ever did while you were alive."

Then a horrible thought manifested itself to Julee:

"I'm dead, aren't I? Oh God, how did it happen? I'm dead. I must be!"

"Nearly," Seth said once more, "but not quite. Your drink was spiked by the guy with the greasy hair and piggy eyes at the bar. He won't remember doing it though; I had to work through him to arrange this meeting. Don't worry, my dear, Reet won't leave you alone so you're quite safe. He'll have to get his kicks elsewhere."

"I'm safe from him," Julee said scornfully, "but am I safe from you?"

"Yes. I've been accidentally conjured. I recognise the irony in this. I want you to hear me out before you say anything else, OK. You must listen to me."

Seth's aura seemed to bleed outwards. Many colours of

vibrant light started to swim around his outline, the result of which made Julee lightheaded.

"This is why I gave up the booze," Julee said miserably.

"I was murdered," Seth raged. "The spell backfired. This is the result."

"This has to be a dream..." Julee formed the sentence only to be cut off by Seth.

"THIS IS NOT A DREAM!"

"It *must* be a dream!" Julee replied, her voice uneven. "The police found your body a few days ago on the cliffs. Your granny came to town to identify you."

"I bet the old dingbat threw a tea party to celebrate my death!"

"Then she only did what I'm going to do when I get back to The Cottage!"

Seth reacted by mouthing a secret silent spell. Suddenly his bleeding aura detonated into a supernova of hot light. The glare burned Julee's eyes with an intensity she had never thought possible. It felt like she'd stared into the sun for ten minutes straight without blinking. Only one thought looped endlessly through Julee's head, one thought that kept her sane in the fury of the lights:

('This is a dream this is a dream this is a dream.')

The haze of light that was Seth zipped behind Julee where it rematerialized into human form again, atoms rearranging efficiently with other atoms until the dreadfully familiar features of Seth came into view again. If this was an attempt to impress or intimidate Julee, it was all for nothing, because she quickly recovered from Seth's ghostly party piece.

Julee spun around to face Seth as an equal.

"Stupid bitch!" Seth screeched. "I am ensnared between different dimensions."

"Who killed you?" Julee demanded to know.

"Didn't you listen to that psychic earlier?" Seth cried out. "He gave you and Reet a clue. You must listen to him even if he looks like a dodgy gameshow host."

The sound of Julee's laughter echoed throughout the empty club.

"You mean to tell me he's actually for real?"

"Is any of this real?" Seth said. "Maybe we're all dreaming the same dream?"

"He told us some weird stuff today..."

"What exactly did he say?" Seth demanded. "I must know!"

Julee's thoughts were sluggish and undefined, she tried to remember exactly what Campbell said, but when she spoke them aloud, the words scared her:

"He told us you completed the spell, you managed to call The Infinite."

"Yes," Seth said gloomily, "but it didn't go the way I expected. It's paradoxical that in death, I finally realised where I had been going wrong with the ritual before. What happened on Halloween wasn't my fault. Coryn was right for once. There was someone else in the forest with us that night."

Julee didn't reply. She wasn't quite ready to talk about Halloween yet.

"You remember what I told you in the forest. You know what happens when someone successfully conjures The Infinite."

Julee remembered Seth's explanation on Halloween with an undercurrent of alarm.

"The Infinite sends three Ambassadors down from the higher dimensions."

Seth didn't reply. He didn't have to say a word. The look on his face was enough.

"How long do we have before The Ambassadors get here?"

"Not long," Seth said flatly, "I need you to do something for me before they arrive."

"What?" Julee asked suspiciously.

"You must complete the ritual and free me from this interdimensional prison."

"You're mad!" Julee yelled. "I'm not contacting The Infinite. I wouldn't dare!"

Seth, confounded by Julee's lack of obedience, confessed something shocking.

"Someone else in The Cottage has already attempted the ritual."

"After what happened on Halloween? Are they mad?"

But Seth didn't seem to hear her, his rage had brought about a nonsensical rant.

"I got closer to The Infinite than they ever will. I am the only servant The Infinite needs in this universe! The eyes of the sky opened for me, Julee, and then it was all taken away. I became the sacrifice and that shouldn't have happened. Now the spell will unleash terrible consequences until The Ambassadors leave this world."

Julee could hear the sound of bass in the distance. The nightclub was returning to normal. She was returning to the real world and she felt elated by that revelation.

"You must give me access to your mind," Seth cried out, "let me control you!"

"Get lost, Seth!" Julee yelled. "You stay the hell out of my head!"

"Then I'll have to go for someone else..." Seth giggled snidely.

Julee threw her hands up protectively and threw herself away from the phantom in front of her. She denied him. She denied his existence. She denied the experience. She fled Seth and followed the sound of the bass beats back into reality until she awoke to see Reet's face hanging over her. She looked terrified.

"You collapsed!" Reet babbled. "I thought you were dead."

"Nearly," Julee said in a shaky voice, "but not quite."

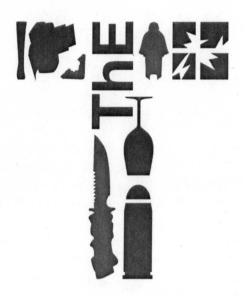

BLACK FOREST GATEAU
After The Funeral

Disappointed by the lack of dessert due to abrupt dinner cancellation, Lawrence decided to raid the well-stocked fridge in the kitchen. There was a Black Forest gateau in that fridge and Lawrence was determined to scoff it all. After a few minutes Jack sauntered into the kitchen with cake on his mind too. Jack never, ever walked. He always sauntered with a confident strut Lawrence often tried to imitate.

Jack laughed as soon as he caught sight of his friend sneakily eating the pudding, which led to Lawrence joining in with his amusement. Despite his easy laughter, the cake was delicious, and Lawrence secretly hoped Jack didn't want a slice of it.

"I decided I didn't want to skip dessert," Lawrence said amiably.

"Me too," Jack said agreeably, "I'm a growing man with needs. I might have the leftover sausage hotpot from Wednesday night. There's some left in the fridge."

"Everything you eat goes into your arms," Lawrence said with a pang of envy.

Jack flexed his big arms. They were his pride and joy. After another quick flex, he walked over and seized a slice of cake from Lawrence, stuffing it into his mouth before his friend could protest.

Lawrence shook his head, stifling more laughter, then said:

"You're a dick sometimes!"

Jack's rude reply was inaudible because his mouth was full of Black Forest gateau.

Lily was with Mother in her office. The care workers, all of whom would probably quit their jobs tomorrow, had abandoned The Cottage for the safety of their homes. Mother was stressed beyond her usual measure as a result. She didn't even bother learning the names of her staff anymore because turnover was so appallingly high.

The two psychologists were engaged in a heated debate over The Abomination. Her presence at The Cottage was causing more problems, but Lily suspected the real reason Mother was upset was because Patricia had kicked off during Seth's memorial.

"Patricia's parents don't want her!" Lily repeated again. She felt that was the only thing she said during the whole conversation. "She's too dangerous to put into a care home and the asylum has no spare rooms. She has to stay here in The Cottage."

Mother stood up and furiously paced around her office. She stopped and turned to Lily, her face pitched between decision and indecision. Then she started pacing again until she finally reached a verdict:

"This is not up for debate, Lily. Patricia goes as soon as possible."

Lily didn't offer any resistance. She knew Mother wouldn't bother listening to anything she had to say anyway. Her thoughts were also sidetracked by Julee's earlier conversation with Coryn, the tail end of which she had caught when she had entered the conservatory. They had been talking about Seth, but what exactly had they been saying? The teenagers were being maddeningly enigmatic tonight. First they refused to discuss Halloween and now this. It was all very conspiratorial to Lily.

"Are you listening to me?" Mother's voice cut into Lily's clouded thoughts.

"Of course I'm listening!" Lily said defensively.

"I want you to make preparations to have Patricia transferred out of here."

"I think you're making a mistake. She needs our help."

"She needs an armed guard!" Mother said hotly.

(Silence)

"Can I leave now?" Lily asked between gritted teeth.

Mother's response was a curt, "Of course."

Lawrence and Jack were talking about girls. Specifically, they were talking about Reet.

"She called me baldy," Lawrence said despondently.

"You *are* a baldy though!" Jack laughed.

"I know that!" Lawrence retorted as they left the kitchens and headed for the spiral staircase. "But Reet has never been nasty to me. She's been different since Seth died. I'm really worried about her, Jack."

"Well," Jack gorged on the last of his cake as he climbed the stairs, "she's probably a bit stressed. Don't take it personally."

"Even her voice sounded different! She's *never* spoken to me like that."

Jack suddenly thrust his hand out and stopped Lawrence in mid-step. He pointed his index finger towards the end of the long hallway, frantically stabbing the air with it. Lawrence followed the direction of Jack's moving finger towards a wide open door that shouldn't have been wide open at all.

"There's someone in Seth's room," Jack whispered gruffly.

"But…why?"

Jack shrugged his bafflement. He honestly didn't know why anybody would want to break into Seth's bedroom, but the idea made him uncomfortable regardless.

"What if they're still in there?" Lawrence wondered aloud.

"There's only one way to find out," Jack replied.

"What?"

But Lawrence already knew what Jack was going to say.

"We go inside and look for ourselves."

"I shouldn't have asked," Lawrence said miserably.

The two housemates were so caught up by the mystery of the open door that they failed to notice another normally locked door was wide open. The intruder had quickly moved from Seth's bedroom and was now hiding inside The Abomination's.

And they had a very special mission in mind for Patricia…

"Patricia!" a voice called out into the fog. "Wake up, Patricia!"

Patricia's eyes flickered open but she couldn't keep them like that, because whilst her medication made her body heavy, they made her mind light and wavy.

"Wake up, idiot!" The voice snapped impatiently. "Before Jack and Lawrence find me in here!"

Patricia recognised the voice but the face behind the voice wouldn't come to her thoughts. Suddenly the restraints binding her arms and legs slackened off.

"I'm releasing you from your jail," the voice said with delight, "but there is a condition for your freedom. It comes at a price. Do you want to pay the price?"

Suddenly Patricia realised her eyes were no longer heavy, the drugs and medication had lost their power over her. The voice had indeed released her from the bed. Patricia felt a strong urge to rise up and smash everything into tiny bits. But what could she smash? Everything in her room had been wrecked in her last tantrum. Patricia began to panic as she realised there was nothing left to smash!

"They call you The Abomination. You must hurt them, Patricia. Hurt them bad."

Patricia suddenly realised she didn't need to smash objects, she could smash people instead. She really, really wanted to smash people up and see what happened.

"Julee suspects the truth of things!" the voice said as it left the room. "She has to be silenced. Julee laughs at you the most, Patricia. Why don't you teach her a lesson for laughing at you? Hurt her, Patricia. Hurt Julee bad!"

Patricia stood up from her bed and roared triumphantly. Then she drew her fist back and put it straight through the nearest window. After breaking the glass, Patricia studied her knuckles with childlike wonder, but she soon grew tired of this. She stumbled out of her room in search of something or someone to smash.

But by then her liberator had already slipped out of the room and back downstairs with the others. The secrets in Seth's bedroom could wait until later.

LAWRENCE AND HOW HE LOST HIS HAIR

"Hurry up, Lawrence! We're going to be late for the cinema."
   Lawrence leaned out of his bedroom door and shouted,
   "I'm brushing my hair!"
   And everybody laughed.

It was the first thing people noticed about Lawrence Anderson. It also happened to be the first thing they asked him about. His lack of hair seemed to obsess people in a way that genuinely puzzled Lawrence. It didn't matter to him, because he had lived his life for so long without hair that he couldn't bring himself to care.

It was, Lawrence thought, only hair and lots of people crop their hair for fashion.

But the questions unnerved Lawrence anyway, because he knew people could see the truth behind his happy-go-lucky smiles. He hadn't always been bald; he'd had hair once upon a time, a glorious thatch of curly blond hair in fact. He knew this because he'd seen photographs of his first day at nursery.

He remembered adults at the nursery commenting on his hair, how lovely it had looked, the gorgeous blond mane he used to have and then...

Then Uncle Joseph moved into his house.

"I want you to say hello to your Uncle Joseph," Carol Anderson said.

"Where's Uncle Eric?" Lawrence asked.

"He's run off with Aunt Tracy."

Little Lawrence Anderson, still with a glorious mane of hair, petted his lip and tried not to cry. His Mum didn't like him crying and she threatened to beat him if he started. It was difficult for Lawrence though, because he really liked his Uncle Eric. Eric would take him out to play football when his Mum had a headache at the weekend. Lawrence tried to remember life before his Uncle Eric, but all he could remember was a man called Uncle Mike. Lawrence liked him too. He was funny and used to dance around the living room to Kylie Minogue.

"Don't bother asking about your Uncle Mike," Carol said bitterly, "he's run off with your Uncle Connor."

All Lawrence could think about was, "Who is Uncle Connor?"

And then he burst into tears and ran up to his bedroom to find Pooh Bear, hoping he could escape Mum's misdirected wrath. He couldn't, of course.

Lily tapped her pen against the file sitting on her desk. Lawrence smiled bashfully as she smiled at him. Pretty girls didn't tend to smile or pay any kind of attention to Lawrence, but he still tried to impress them anyway. He loved these improvised sessions with Lily, because he got to talk to her alone, even though he couldn't really tell her what she needed to know. It wasn't his fault though. Lawrence genuinely couldn't remember huge parts of his own life. The unimportant details were easy to recall but the big things were hazy and imprecise.

"I remember things differently in my head every time I think about the past. Sometimes I see it one way, sometimes another. It's always a multiple choice exam, remembering my history. Do you what I mean?"

Lily nodded and scribbled more notes. She had noticed something very interesting about her patient; every time Lawrence spoke about his past his hand moved up and touched his head nervously.

"What age were you when your hair fell out?" Lily asked quietly.

"Oh," Lawrence replied, "That I do remember..."

Uncle Joseph didn't take Lawrence to the football pitch, but he did take him fishing, a past-time Lawrence loved more than football. His little arms weren't able to hold the rod steadily, but Uncle Joseph taught him how to catch and reel the fish.

"You get the fish and then we get our picture taken if it's a big one!"

"Why?" Little Lawrence asked quizzically.

"Because that's what you do! That's what my dad taught me."

Little Lawrence glowed with happiness at Uncle Joseph's words.

The rod went taught as a fish bit into the bait.

Lily didn't want to push Lawrence any further. His face glistened with a slick layer of sweat, brought on by unwanted memories.

She knew fine well the story would change at next week's session, but she had an uneasy feeling that perhaps one of the many, many tales Lawrence had told her during their sessions might be the truth. She jotted this theory into the little red diary sitting on her lap.

It wasn't merely a diary; it was an extension of Lily's thoughts.

"What happened next?"

Carol Anderson wasn't very attractive anymore. Whenever Lawrence looked at her, he struggled to see exactly what others saw in her, because she was overweight and her face was bright orange. Too many sun beds and ecstasy pills had ruined her features and transformed her into a haggard mess of a woman.

"This is your fault!" Carol screamed furiously.

"It's not my fault you look like a dried-up old Oompa Loompa!"

"No man stays with me because I've got a little leech sucking all my money and life. Who wants to waste time with a single mother?"

"Uncle Joseph left because you cheated on him with his best mate. You've only got yourself to blame."

Lawrence was running a bath because the shower had broken down, but his Mum was sitting on the toilet seat, drunk and upset. He couldn't shift her so he decided to go for a bath and hope she would leave the bathroom.

No such luck, unfortunately.

"When will you die?" Lawrence's Mum shouted hoarsely.

"When will you get a job?"

Carol stood up, swaying unsteadily on her feet, and she stumbled across the bathroom towards her son. He turned away from her to lean down and check the water in the bathtub. This was a grave mistake on his part.

Eighteen stones of furious drunk slammed into Lawrence and sent him downwards into the roasting hot water. His first instinct was to jump out of the bath, away from the boiling liquid, but his Mum had other ideas and she carried out her assault with lethal accuracy.

Her hands clawed into Lawrence's hair and pushed his head forward towards the tub. He tried yelling at her to stop, but she was too heavy and too powerful for his scrawny frame to resist.

"Letgoofmeorillkickyourheadin!" Lawrence yelled, but to no avail.

Carol shoved her son's head right into the tub and the roasting water. She kept him down deep in the wet depths and didn't let him up until his body went limp.

"My hair fell out later on that night." Lawrence's eyes were wide but there were no tears in them. He never, ever cried. "Mother thinks I've got some kind of post-traumatic stress disorder that stops my hair coming back. Nobody knows for sure."

For the first time ever, Lily found herself in agreement with Mother.

USEFUL THINGS TO DO WITH HOTPOT
After The Funeral

The sight of Seth's bedroom in the gloom was an unnerving one for Jack.

"It hasn't changed a bit since I was last here," he whispered hoarsely.

This came as a surprise to Lawrence, who had no idea Jack was on such friendly terms with Seth. He couldn't believe anyone could be friends with Seth.

"When were you here?"

"A few weeks ago." Jack walked around Seth's king-size bed, towards a chest of drawers, which he rested his hand upon. It came away with a thin layer of dust on it.

"It's weird to think he's dead. He's really dead and ain't coming back."

"Yes," Lawrence said as his eyes darted nervously around the room.

"Someone was in here," Jack said calmly, "but they heard us coming up the stairs and got spooked. But where did they go? It had to be another room on this level otherwise we would have spotted them."

Lawrence seemed to consider something else.

"There's something I don't understand about all of this," he said.

"What?"

"Why would someone want to break into Seth's room? What's in here for them?"

Jack had to give way to Lawrence's logic. He turned and looked down at the chest of drawers and noticed one of them was partially open. Before Jack could open it up fully and see what was inside, he was startled by the sound of an animal roaring.

Then he heard the sound of a window being punched through.

"Patricia!" Jack and Lawrence both said at once.

Mother was standing in the living room by the fireplace, attempting to stoke some life into the fire, when she felt a silhouette passing over her. The glow from the fire illuminated and enhanced it into enormous proportions. Mother knew the shadow belonged to The Abomination before she even turned around, because only Patricia could put forth a shadow that size.

She cautiously twisted around, keenly aware at how exposed she was without any of the care workers by her side, but Mother also knew it was unsafe to show fear. She would take command of the situation and show Patricia that intimidation did not work at The Cottage. Mother would resolve this incident quickly and efficiently.

Mother didn't even get a chance to speak. Patricia launched her into the air with a mighty backhand slap. She was out cold before she even hit the nearby wall.

"Sausages..." Patricia giggled maniacally.

Julee made it to the living room before everybody else, which was bad luck on her part.

Patricia turned and caught sight of Julee and her childlike mind suddenly felt a surge of hate. This hatred translated into action: Patricia flew straight for Julee.

"Hurricane Patricia is on the way!" Julee screamed as she ran for her life.

Coryn was halfway down the stairs, wondering where all the noise was coming from, when she spotted The Abomination's destructive pursuit of Julee. She turned without saying a word and ran back up the staircase towards the safety of her bedroom. She didn't reach her destination, however, because Reet stood in her way.

SMACK! They collided into each other.

"Phone the police!" Julee's voice cried from downstairs. "Phone the SWAT team!"

Jack ran past a dazed Reet and Coryn. He held a green baseball bat in his hands, which he proceeded to swing violently in every direction.

Lawrence split from Jack and bolted into Mother's office, grabbing the nearest telephone. He violently jabbed the keypad until the operator answered his call. It took him a few seconds to form the words necessary to bring reinforcements to The Cottage.

"Get an ambulance up here too!" Lawrence cried.

When Lawrence left Mother's office, he found both Coryn and Reet had recovered from their accident, and both were rushing downstairs with Lily. He nearly laughed out loud when he found Lily toting a weapon. But it wasn't a baseball bat. It was a fire extinguisher, which she held in her hands like a magick talisman. He doubted that a mere fire extinguisher could ward away The Abomination.

Lawrence suddenly realised that Julee had stopped screaming.

Jack crept into the kitchen with a cautious step, his bat held high above his head. He wasn't afraid to use a weapon; in fact his temper had gotten him into trouble more times than he could remember. He hoped Julee wasn't too badly hurt, he vowed to use the bat repeatedly on Patricia if she harmed Julee in any way...

Julee stepped out from beside the fridge, making Jack jump slightly. He was relieved to see she wasn't hurt or marked in any way, which made him wonder what exactly had happened to Patricia. When he looked around the rest of the kitchen, his question was quickly answered; sitting on the floor was Patricia, greedily slobbering on the remains of a sausage hotpot. The empty bowl was discarded on the floor, useless.

"She was about to rip my face off when I had a brainwave," Julee said happily.

"You gave her the hotpot!"

"She kept shouting at me and I remembered the leftovers. Pity its cold."

They stood there together watching Patricia eating the cold leftovers with great gusto. Jack felt a strange urge to take Julee's hand in his own, but he didn't get a chance. Lily ('damn her' Jack thought) walked into the kitchen to deliver some news:

"There's something wrong with Mother. I've tried all the First Aid I know, but nothing is working. An ambulance is on the way."

Lily turned and left the kitchen to rejoin the others, but not before she gave Patricia a look filled with a desolate significance.

SETH'S (UNUSUAL) PART-TIME JOB

Every Wednesday, without fail, Lily treated herself to an afternoon of pampering.

It was necessary for her to do this if only because her work at The Cottage left her stressed and drained. She relished the opportunity to get her nails polished, her face rubbed, and her hair trimmed into a fashionable style. Her job at The Cottage meant she was always in reach of the local beauty salon, which came in useful when she had some spare time to herself. Spare time in The Cottage was like gold dust to Lily.

Lily's favourite part of her weekly beauty regime was Madame Katia Alexandrina's nail-buffing routine. A Polish migrant and a cosmetic genius, Lily wouldn't trust her nails to anybody else. Katia could work miracles out of mediocre material and every Wednesday she effortlessly turned Lily's nails from drab to fab.

One afternoon, whilst chatting away to an unusually unfocused Katia, Lily decided to put her training into use once again in order to get her favourite nail technician to open up about her problems. It was this direct approach that got results in the end.

"You haven't buffed my nails to your usual standard. Are you okay, Katia?"

"I am so sorry," Katia said with a red face.

Lily waved her free hand forgivingly. Then she realised her nail polish hadn't completely dried, so she frantically waved her hand a few times more.

"It's not your fault, Katia. Something is obviously on your mind. Remember, I *am* a trained psychologist. If you have problems, you *must* share them with me."

"Well," Madame said in a voice thick with worry, "Someone has been sending me poison pen letters. They are really horrible. I do not think I can take it anymore!"

Katia's face broke and her hidden worry was finally set free after months of secrecy.

"I am being blackmailed," she sobbed, all attempts at nail buffing abandoned.

Lily sighed deeply. So it wasn't just her getting the menacing mail then.

"You've been sent letters as well?" Lily replied smoothly. "I got a few last week. I just ignored them. They're probably the work of a sociopathic repressive with a particularly vicious malaise and far too much time on his hands."

"I do not know who is doing this to me!" Katia cried out tearfully. "Why would someone be so mean for no reason? Patrick at the Post Office has been sent some nasty letters too."

"Working in the Post Office, Peter is bound to receive lots of letters."

Katia smiled weakly at Lily's little joke, but the tears quickly started again.

"I know at least five more who have been sent letters by the blackmailer!"

Lily took Katia's hand and smiled a most reassuring smile.

"I'm positive I know who's behind this. I'm going to have a word with him..."

When Lily arrived back at The Cottage, she went straight to her office to check if the security measures she had installed were still in place. She craned her neck down the side of the door and noticed the little piece of string at the bottom was still unbroken. Satisfied that Seth hadn't broken into her office again, Lily unlocked the door and entered quietly into her private domain.

The letters on her desk were neatly typed in identical Book Antiqua font, but the messages were all very different. Some were menacing while others were simply spiteful. They threatened dire action if she didn't do as she was told. Lily didn't care about the letters; they were all useful additions to the psychiatric file she was compiling on Seth Kevorkian. It didn't matter if Seth had discovered something about her that she didn't want anyone else to know. The time would come when his threats would mean nothing anyway. That time would be soon.

What she hadn't expected was that Seth Kevorkian would also extend his baleful influence from out with The Cottage and into the village. Katia had shown her some of his more colourful blackmail letters during her nail buffing, and she found them objectionable and vindictive.

(Seth, it transpired, had somehow discovered that Katia's sisters had come over with their husbands from Poland. Two of them had prior convictions back home for some undisclosed crime. Seth's intentions to report Katia would, according to his venomous notes, come to nothing if she paid him five hundred pounds in cash.)

"What an evil brat," Lily said loudly.

The sound of laughter drifted upstairs towards Lily's office. Seth's laughter was easily identifiable, because it was obnoxious and earsplitting. He wanted the world to know he was having all the fun. But Seth would probably laugh in a crowd of manic depressives just to let them know how much fun he was having in life, even if that wasn't necessarily the case.

Lily picked up her telephone and called downstairs, waiting for a care assistant to answer. It was swiftly picked up and she uttered eight words in a strident voice:

"I want Seth here in my office now."

As if by magick, Seth appeared in Lily's office. He looked faintly amused.

"That was quick," Lily said, disturbed by the unnerving speed of Seth's arrival. She already knew Seth had made himself rather comfortable in her office many times before. She kept this knowledge to herself, waiting for the best time to speak it.

"May I be seated?" Seth asked as he pulled out a chair and sat down

Lily didn't speak, she was content to sit and watch his expression, study his posture, examine his whole persona. She had been trained in how to read body language, a skill which came in very useful to a psychologist. Lily could almost tell what a person was thinking just by examining the movements of their body; twitchy eyes, a stray glance, a furtive smile…they could all be used to see whether or not a person was lying.

"What do you want with me?" Seth asked in his usual insolent tone. He ignorantly started looking through a stack of books Lily kept on her desk: *Psychology for Allied Health Professionals*, *Psychological Problems and Their Solutions*, *A Handbook of Adult Clinical Psychology*, *Necronomicon*, *The Psychology of the Elderly* and many more on a variety of subjects.

Lily grinded her teeth together, because her first instinct was to stand up and strike Seth right on his face. But she would lose her job and that wouldn't be worth the small moment of pleasure smacking Seth would surely bring her. She had too much to do at The Cottage, and the boy sitting before her had it in him to ruin her plans.

So Lily controlled herself and asked a very simple question. Her blunt demeanor meant her question took Seth by surprise:

"Did you post threatening letters to Katia Alexandrina?"

Eight heartbeats later...

"No," Seth replied frostily. "I don't know what you're talking about."

(A not quite concealed smile, slight dilation of his pupils, minor clenching of the palms. These apparently unrelated things meant nothing, but together they laid bare Seth's lies before Lily's trained eyes.)

"You're a liar!" Lily slammed her fists down on her desk.

"Oh," Seth cackled vociferously, "I forgot that you can read body language."

Lily might have let this slip past her, but Seth's words were heavy with meaning.

"How the hell did you know that?" Lily shouted angrily.

Suddenly, without any other prompting, the sinister significance behind Seth's words came to Lily in a colossal flash of logical lucidity. He had been in her office again, sneaking through her private files, looking at things he shouldn't.

"How dare you!" Lily could barely speak, such was her anger. "I've warned you about going through my personal things! I know you've been looking for my diary. You'd better watch yourself, Seth Kevorkian! Stay out of my office!"

Seth erupted into girlish laughter. He was clearly entertained by something Lily had just said to him. Some sort of implicit truth between the two that went unspoken, but it didn't need to be said out loud, because Lily knew exactly what Seth was implying. She decided to let him know in no uncertain terms that she wouldn't be intimidated by his jibes and catty comments.

"I mean it," Lily snapped, "I won't allow you to continue with this foolishness."

Seth stifled a melodramatic yawn, a classic gambit to lull Lily into a false sense of security, but she wasn't deceived by this tactic, for Lily knew every trick Seth had in his arsenal. How? Because unbeknownst to Mother and everybody else at The Cottage, Lily had already gone through Seth's personal files whilst compiling her own on him, a task which had proved rather informative.

A clash of wills between the psychologist and the aspiring warlock took place in the little office, a battle that didn't result in a decisive victory for either person.

"I want you to stop sending out these letters," Lily said softly, dangerously.

"Give me your special red diary," Seth replied with equivalent menace, "and I won't come near your...office."

The mocking way in which he uttered the word 'office' imbued the word with an entirely new significance. Once more Lily didn't appreciate what he was getting at, so she allowed herself the indulgence of a snigger. Seth's barefaced greed didn't come as a surprise to Lily; his desperation to read her diary was something to be pitied.

"You'll never read my diary. Oh, and I know what you did with Coryn's diary. Sticking someone's private thoughts on public display isn't funny or clever. Coryn was distraught because of your handiwork. What is it with you and other people's private property? Why don't you keep your nose out of my business? One of these days you'll annoy the wrong person and get what you deserve."

Seth laughed at Lily's self-righteous indignation. The idea that Seth could put her diary up on public display secretly terrified Lily, and her discomfort seemed to give Seth more power. She could see he actually enjoyed making people ill at ease.

"If you give me your diary, I'll stop writing the letters. Every penny I earn comes from those idiots down in the village. It's very lucrative, Lily. You're asking me to give up the equivalent of a part-time job."

"I am not asking you to stop sending the letters." Lily punctuated every word with a wave of her index finger, "I am *telling* you to stop sending the letters."

Lily stopped pointing at Seth to examine her nail, it looked a bit frayed, and then she remembered the disappointing job Katia did on it earlier that day.

"What will you do if I don't stop?" Seth asked sweetly.

"I'll restrict your movements here in The Cottage. I'll stop you leaving here."

Seth seemed to actually consider what Lily had said to him.

"Okay," he said amiably, "I know when I'm beaten. You can tell Katia and all the others that the blackmail letters are going to stop. There will be no more."

Lily was pleasantly surprised by the swiftness of Seth's defeat. She had expected him to fight back with more viciousness than he did, and a small part of her felt real disappointment at the speedy outcome.

At least Katia will be able to do my nails properly, Lily thought absent-mindedly.

When Lily looked up, she discovered Seth was gone, effectively vanishing out of her office as smoothly as he had appeared.

"As if by magick," Lily muttered to herself.

Then she checked her safe to see if her little red diary was still safely inside, which it was, to her deep relief.

Katia's little sister was arrested the day after Lily's confrontation with Seth. As a result of the arrest, she was charged with illegal entry into the country and deported back to Poland.

Seth denied his involvement in this incident but Lily didn't believe him.

LILY GETS A PROMOTION
After The Funeral

The ambulance arrived swiftly and two paramedics examined Mother's unconscious body with precision and understanding. She wasn't dead, thankfully, just concussed. The blow delivered to her at the hands of The Abomination had knocked her out and she had to go to hospital as a result. Only in a fully equipped hospital could she be given a proper examination.

Lily elected to remain behind to look after everybody.

"I'm in charge of The Cottage now," she said quietly, "the responsibility to keep you all safe falls to me. I am Mother's second in command, after all."

(Julee, weirdly enough, didn't feel safe in the least. But no-one else spoke up so she remained discreet in her insecurities.)

When the police arrived for Patricia, Reet found to her horror that one of the officers was none other than Sergeant McAllister. She tried to melt away into the little group of housemates huddled near the main door, but she was spotted and the policeman raised a quizzical eyebrow in her direction.

A few minutes passed before Patricia was hauled out of the kitchen by the police; she offered no resistance and sluggishly followed them without saying a word. As she walked across the hallway towards the waiting police cars outside, she looked around at the housemates and waved sorrowfully at them.

"I hope Mother's alright," Reet said as Lily closed and locked the doors.

Lily flashed her most reassuring smile at Reet.

"I'm sure she'll be fine, it's a mild case of concussion, but the doctors will still need to thoroughly check up on her anyway."

The little group started walking down the grand hallway only to be confronted by the large portrait of Seth Kevorkian. His dark curled hair looked better in the photo than it did in real life. Reet felt a strange sense of fascination with the picture, his eyes especially were magnetic, but they weren't the only eyes on her. Reet turned to find Lawrence staring intensely at her. She gave him a wink.

"It seems really unlikely, doesn't it?" Jack spoke but his voice was absentminded.

"What does?" Julee didn't take her eyes away from the huge smiling picture. The more she studied the canvas, the more repulsed she felt by it, the fake smile which suddenly looked mocking rather than happy.

"It seems unlikely that Seth would be killed so easily."

"It wasn't easy though," Reet answered Jack's point, "he was shot in the chest several times. It must have been horrible for him. What a way to go! Yuck."

Lily didn't want to hear the morbid discourse, so she left the little group to stand by the painting and continue their unappealing tribute to Seth.

She wasn't even halfway through the dining room when the doorbell chimed across the house, loud and shrill, it was completely unanticipated.

Who could it be? Lily wondered.

Coryn's excited voice called into the dining room:

"I'll answer it!"

"If it's a salesman, tell him we don't want anything!" Lily shouted as she sped into the hallway, directly in front of the main doors.

"It won't be a salesman at this time of night," Julee muttered.

Coryn opened one of the double doors just in time for Lily to skid across the laminate flooring of the hall and stop next to her. The door opened to reveal…

A man. He stood there, battered by powerful winds, looking faintly ridiculous in a black tailored coat, a silver cravat around his neck. In his hands he held what looked like a laptop bag. His knuckles were white with the effort of not letting the bag become victim of the heavy wind storm.

"Who the heck are you?" Lily asked abruptly, her famously sarcastic tone in play.

Julee and Reet looked at each other in shock. They knew precisely the identity of the strange man standing in their doorway. They had visited his shop recently.

"Campbell Devine!" the two girls cried out in unison.

"The end of today starts tomorrow," Campbell announced cheerily. "Or does the end of tomorrow start today? Seeing into the future can get very confusing."

He crossed the threshold into the hall of The Cottage without waiting for permission. Lily didn't like that because she considered such an action to be disrespectful. She was prepared to expel the strange intruder, but he faced her down with a glare that stopped the words forming in her throat.

"Someone in this house shot Seth Kevorkian," Campbell said melodramatically.

Lily was speechless for the first time in her entire life.

RUMOURS OF THE INFINITE

When Campbell Whitmore left school, he didn't know which profession he should take up. He had absolutely no talent whatsoever and his exam results were utterly calamitous. But Campbell was impelled onward by one simple ambition; to make as much money as possible with as little physical effort as he could manage.

It didn't take Campbell long to choose psychic consultancy as his ideal career. It looked ridiculously easy to him, possibly the easiest job in the whole world! All he had to do was tell the downtrodden twits exactly what they wanted to hear, before relieving them of their hard earned cash.

There was, however, a slight flaw in Campbell's strategy. A devastating kink in the masterplan that was as unlikely as it was frustrating:

Every prediction he made came true!

He would sit at the desk in his poky bedsit, dreaming up preposterous fibs, only to watch them unfold before his own eyes over the following months. Even the most implausible predictions came to pass! Campbell nearly fainted when his most ludicrous vision came true; it was The One with the Famous American Sitcom actress turned Movie Star winning an Oscar. There she was two months later, standing tall on a stage, holding her Oscar aloft with pride and poise. Not even the most powerful psychic could have predicted that one and yet Campbell had effortlessly plucked this future event out of thin air.

Campbell decided to use his new-found powers wisely. He took out a loan and set up a little business in a provincial constituency. He eventually settled on Castlecrankie Village, because he knew it was full of superstitious types with little sense and lots of money. The location of his shop was prime real estate, being directly across from a pub called The Devil's Dumplings. His next step was to erase his past and change his name from Whitmore to the jazzier sounding Devine, which felt more peculiar and elegant. Under the guise of Campbell Devine, he predicted the future with unerring accuracy for hundreds of happy customers.

Life was going splendidly for Campbell Devine until the day Seth Kevorkian walked through his shop doors for a psychic reading.

Campbell looked into Seth's soul and his head was filled with horror.

Seth looked very sullen, slightly suspicious and even a little bit bemused. Seth's luxurious thick and curly hair brought out a slight streak of envy in Campbell because his own hair was beginning to thin at the top. Campbell's tightening hairline was the true reason he wore a wizard's hat during business hours. Not that he would ever admit that to anyone…

"Can I help you, Seth?" Campbell asked in his overdramatic Irish accent.

"Yes," Seth said calmly, "you can stop speaking in that stupid fake accent."

"Thank God!" Campbell replied immediately. Far from being insulted, he was actually rather relieved. "They always expect it, you know, my customers. Some of them tell me I sound like Merlin, so that might be the reason I speak in that Irish accent. But then how do they know what Merlin sounded like? He's dead isn't he? Did he even exist except as a bearded scruff on TV?"

Seth grinned, somewhat taken aback that his usually rude temperament had brought out a much different reaction from normal. His unpleasant manner was a means of testing people for resistance, but he found himself rather taken by Campbell Devine. Seth looked around his shop with a keen interest, studying it methodically.

Campbell, meanwhile, continued to keep an eye on Seth, watching carefully as his new customer stalked around the room, looking over the stack of tarot card books like some kind of government inspector.

Seth stopped his inspection of the shop and faced Campbell with a sober expression. When he spoke again, it was with a surprised tone of voice:

"You're actually for real, aren't you?"

Whatever tests Campbell had been under with Seth, it seemed he had passed them with flying colours. He didn't quite know how to answer that question, so he did it with complete honesty. For some reason Campbell felt a keen respect for this person standing before him: he had an aura of unspeakable power and potential.

"Yes." Campbell took a seat at his little wooden desk. "I can see the future."

Seth darted forward and punched the desk with enough force to wobble it. Campbell didn't flinch; he merely moved his eyes slowly up onto Seth's face.

"You knew my name as soon as I walked into your crummy shop!" Seth hissed exultantly. "I didn't even introduce myself and yet you knew my name."

Campbell didn't mean to do that, but it happened more often than he liked.

"It creeps out my customers," he replied in a joyless tone of voice.

"How do you know the future?" Seth didn't break eye contact from Campbell.

"I just know."

"Is there magick in my future?" Seth gently took the seat opposite Campbell.

"There's no such thing as magick," Campbell said automatically.

Seth laughed long and loud at Campbell's remark.

"What a pair we are!" he said whilst stifling his laughter. "Don't you see the incongruity of a psychic telling a wannabe warlock that magick isn't real?"

Campbell didn't have a comeback, partly because whatever he said would sound foolish and also because he didn't know what 'incongruity' actually meant.

"We live in a reasonable world which tells us the incredible is impossible," Seth continued enthusiastically, "but reason is about to be swept aside in the new order. I will renovate the universe in my own image! But I need to know if my plan will succeed. You need to tell me the complete truth as you foresee it."

Campbell watched on as Seth pulled a fat wallet out of his satchel. It was stuffed with massive amounts of money, the kind of cash no boy his age could earn lawfully.

"I will read your future," Campbell said as he eyed up a crisp one hundred pound note, "but first I shall power up my tool for divination."

Seth did a restless dance on his chair, failing miserably to hide his excitement.

"What do you use to see the future? Is it a crystal ball? Tarot cards? Tea leaves?"

Campbell Devine shook his head in response to Seth's suggestions.

"No," he said, "I use *this* to see the future..."

He then produced from beneath the table a shiny white laptop.

Seth's expression shifted from one of enthusiasm to one of pure astonishment when he caught sight of the laptop. He raised his eyebrows at Campbell Devine.

"You use a laptop computer to look into the future? That's ridiculous!"

Campbell grinned at Seth's disbelief as he pressed the on/off button on the keyboard. He used the short time it took for the processor to power up to explain the purpose of his laptop, and how essential it was in his psychic readings.

"We live in a reasonable world which tells us the incredible is impossible," Campbell repeated smugly. Then, upon seeing Seth's face cloud over in irritation, he added: "I channel the psychic energy through my fingers and type what comes into my mind. My visions are then displayed in front of your eyes. I print off the sheet of paper (which comes at an extra cost) and then you can read the future for yourself."

Seth thought this was the most amazing thing he'd ever heard of: a psychic who used a laptop to predict the future was a fascinating concept to him. It was completely unlike anything he'd read about in his stolen occult books.

Campbell closed his eyes and took a deep breath.

"Are you ready?"

"Yes," Seth said in a tightly controlled voice.

Suddenly, without any kind of warning, the power of the visions took hold of Campbell. His fingers waltzed across the laptop keyboard until, until, until…

Time had passed when Campbell opened his eyes. He was disorientated but soon steadied himself. Then he looked up at his client and everything changed.

Darkness passed across Seth Kevorkian's face and plunged the shop into murky shadow as the future presented itself to Campbell with stark simplicity. He wasn't alone with Seth, he knew there was something else lurking in the shop, and he trailed the shadow with his eyes until he found the source of the odd phenomenon:

Three figures stood directly behind Seth, who seemed to be completely unaware of them. Campbell couldn't see their faces, but he could see their human-like outlines. The trio of shapes seemed to be reaching out, their hands hovering menacingly above Seth's head. They were his destiny and they were waiting for him to summon them.

Campbell Devine screamed at a terror he hadn't experienced in his entire life.

The light returned and the shop shifted back into the familiar and cozy surroundings. Seth looked slightly amused with Campbell's reaction. His eyes flicked back and forth between Campbell and the laptop LCD screen, which was covered in hastily typed words from the psychic reading.

A conquering smile suddenly broke out on Seth's face.

"Don't do it," Campbell said between ragged breaths, "just don't!"

"What did you see?"

"You are tampering with forces that will tilt the world upside down. You must not do it. I am begging you to avoid your current course of action."

"But there isn't such a thing as magick," Seth jibed, "so it won't matter if I Conjure The Infinite and meet with its Ambassadors."

"Your future holds nothing but madness, magick, and murder. Walking this path will lead to your damnation. Mend your ways, Seth. Please don't cast the spell."

Seth didn't frighten easily though, so he took no notice of Campbell's dire warning, other than as a confirmation that he would be successful in his mission.

Campbell Devine wasn't so much surprised by the news of Seth's murder as he was saddened by it. The news proved that Seth obviously hadn't listened to Campbell's caution. Remembering his reading, Campbell decided to go and look at the print-out from the session, just so he could read what it said. He wanted to make some kind of sense out of his jumbled vision, but when he powered up his laptop and clicked into the file, he found it had been similarly affected by the experience.

In a messy arrangement of typos and spelling errors, one sentence had been typed over and over again by Campbell's clairvoyantly inspired fingers. The words made no sense to him, but Campbell knew Seth had clearly understood their significance.

A range of fearful sensations passed through Campbell as his eyes absorbed the exact words as he had typed them:

tHe eYEs Of ThE SkY HaVE oPeneD. tHe eYEs Of ThE SkY HaVE oPeneD. tHe eYEs Of ThE SkY HaVE oPeneD. tHe eYEs Of ThE SkY HaVE oPeneD. tHe eYEs Of ThE SkY HaVE oPeneD. tHe eYEs Of ThE SkY HaVE oPeneD. tHe eYEs OfThE SkY HaVE oPeneD. tHe eYEs Of ThE SkY HaVE oPeneD. tHe eYEs Of ThE SkY HaVE oPeneD. tHe eYEs Of ThE SkY HaVE oPeneD. tHe eYEs Of ThE SkY HaVE oPeneD. tHe eYEs Of ThE SkY HaVE oPeneD. tHe eYEs OfThE SkY HaVE oPeneD. tHe eYEs Of ThE SkY HaVE oPeneD. tHe eYEs Of ThE SkY HaVE oPeneD. tHe eYEs Of ThE SkY HaVE oPeneD. tHe eYEs Of ThE SkY HaVE oPeneD. tHe eYEs Of ThE SkY HaVE oPeneD. tHe eYEs OfThE SkY HaVE oPeneD. tHe eYEs Of ThE SkY HaVE oPeneD. tHe eYEs Of ThE SkY HaVE oPeneD. tHe eYEs Of ThE SkY HaVE oPeneD. tHe eYEs Of ThE SkY HaVE oPeneD. tHe eYEs Of ThE SkY HaVE oPeneD. tHe eYEs OfThE SkY HaVE oPeneD. tHe eYEs Of ThE SkY HaVE oPeneD. tHe eYEs Of ThE SkY HaVE oPeneD. tHe eYEs Of ThE SkY HaVE oPeneD. tHe eYEs Of ThE SkY HaVE oPeneD.

ThE AmBassaDorS ArE On ThEiR waY.

Not long after Campbell examined the page from Seth's psychic evaluation, his laptop started behaving badly. It would randomly switch itself on and off during the early hours of the night. It would blast horrible sounds at him, noises loud enough to rouse him from his sleep. Sometimes the noises sounded like voices. Depriving the laptop of power didn't help matters; it continued to blink sluggishly, displaying Seth's reading across the monitor over and over again. The laptop also refused to load for Campbell's customers, driving them out of the shop in a haze of disappointment. At first Campbell thought it was a virus, but his powers told him it was a sign. Visions were presented to him, prophecies forewarning him of Armageddon. These visions told him that something very strange was about to happen, and it all led back to Seth.

Campbell suddenly felt very apprehensive about the coming days and nights.

LILY VERSUS THE LOW-RENT WIZARD
After The Funeral

Lily decided to make the best of a bad situation and give the strange newcomer a quick tour of The Cottage. Reet explained that Campbell was the owner of the psychic consultancy business down in the high street, a fact that did little to dispel Lily's innate distrust of the newcomer. In his favour, he seemed to exhibit a genuine interest in the workings of The Cottage; he informed Lily that he'd heard so much gossip about the place that it was good to finally see the reality.

Every now and then Lily would break into giggles, but she managed to suppress the worst of them because she didn't want to appear unprofessional in front of the newcomer. It was very difficult though. Campbell Devine reminded Lily of a low-rent wizard. In all her years of psychology, she hadn't met anyone quite like him. As she accompanied Campbell into the living room, she considered the idea that he would make a fascinating case study into delusional self-obsessed attention seekers.

Julee, Reet and Lawrence were tagging along with Lily, hanging on every word Campbell spoke. They were completely fascinated by the idiosyncratic little psychic. Jack, however, wasn't interested and had quietly decided to go outside for some fresh air.

He hadn't returned yet.

"Why are you here?" Lily finally asked. Her patience was wearing thin.

"Yes," Julee chimed in after Lily's question, "Why are you here?"

"I'm here because of the newspaper headlines," Campbell said in a hushed voice.

"What newspaper headlines?" Lily demanded.

Campbell suddenly caught sight of the roaring fireplace and let out a shriek of pure joy, then he ran over with his hands outstretched, gently warming them across the flames. His custom-made suit was (thankfully) non-flammable.

"The headlines about the big fight. The stuff about Mother being knocked out by Patricia made for very interesting reading."

"Freaky!" Lawrence cried out.

"That's impossible," Lily hissed, not willing to be caught up in this inanity. "Nobody knows what happened here tonight apart from us, the paramedics and the police. How could you read about it in today's newspaper?"

"Not today's newspaper, I'm talking about tomorrow's newspaper," Campbell Devine continued, as though everyone was missing the obvious. He didn't feel seem quite all there. His thoughts were always slipping back and forth into places that normal minds couldn't access.

"What?" Lily nearly screamed. "That's impossible. How can you read tomorrow's newspaper? It hasn't been printed yet. Heck, it hasn't even been written yet!"

Reet answered this question,

"He's psychic. He can see into the future, remember?"

Reet was absolutely correct. Campbell Devine had indeed used his immense psychic powers to read the headlines in tomorrow's newspapers. His previous predictions regarding Seth had both frightened and worried him, but more than that, these jumbled new visions confused him. So enthralled had Campbell been with tomorrow's headlines that he had done something astonishing. Something he had never, ever done. It would probably make his friends and family faint in shock.

Campbell Devine had closed his shop early. And then set off in the direction of The Cottage.

"We've usually got more people here," Lily announced apologetically as she poured tea into a cup for Campbell, "but all the care workers have gone home and Mother is currently in hospital. So I'm in charge of the lunatics for one night only."

Reet shot Lily a look of sheer loathing for her tactless comment. But Lily didn't seem to notice, being too engrossed in drinking tea with Campbell and discussing his reasons for coming to The Cottage.

The sudden switch to civility was part of Lily's trap. She wanted to let Campbell get comfortable before she went in for the kill:

"You aren't being serious, of course."

Campbell's face registered a look of surprise at Lily's proclamation.

"I'm not being serious about what, exactly?"

"Seeing tomorrow's newspaper headlines with your psychic powers."

Both Reet and Julee sat quietly in the background, cozy on the couch, warmed by the fire. They didn't want to interfere in the collision of philosophies between Lily and Campbell, but the tension was clear to see. Lawrence, meanwhile, hovered alone in the background, keeping a close eye on Reet.

Jack was still elsewhere in The Cottage.

"Do you really want to test my power?" Campbell said sourly.

"Yes!" Lily slammed down the cup without once removing her eyes from Campbell Devine's face. "Yes I dare! I don't believe you're psychic. I think you're a fraud."

"Okay," Campbell said with a cruel smile on his face. "I'll tell you the future. It isn't very good, Lily. I know from tomorrow's headlines that someone in this room will leave The Cottage tonight and never return. Don't ask me why, my visions aren't exactly specific, but I know I'm right."

There was a gasp or two from Reet and Julee.

"But before that comes the freak weather conditions."

"Freak weather conditions?" Reet asked.

"That's what I read. There will be freak weather conditions tonight. You literally won't believe your eyes when that happens. The explanations given in the newspapers are all wrong, of course. But the newspapers usually get it wrong."

Then Campbell lowered his voice into a whisper: "Special guests will appear at The Cottage tonight."

"Special guests?" Julee didn't like the way the word *guests* had been delivered. There was something in Campbell's tone that seemed downbeat as he said the word.

The little psychic sipped his tea before looking around at the housemates in the background. He smiled as he uttered one last prediction. It was *the* prediction.

"The identity of Seth Kevorkian's killer will also be revealed."

Lily's face paled significantly as she absorbed the predictions. She could also see from Julee and Reet's expressions that they believed every word of his prophecies.

"Has anyone seen Jack?" Campbell said quietly as he finished the rest of his tea.

"He's outside having some fresh air," Lawrence replied.

"Oh yes," Campbell smirked, because he knew the truth.

JACK'S GUNS

Jack was barely eight years old when he first lied to the police. His father, a man who went by the nickname of Ratty, coached Jack on exactly what to say and how to act. Too young to understand what the word 'alibi' meant, Jack did as he was told and the police didn't doubt him. What kind of policeman would doubt an innocent child?

"Daddy was here with me," Jack told them in a little voice, just like his dad had taught him. "He read me stories before I went to bed."

Jack only discovered years later that his father got away with murder because of that testimony. He'd been fighting with a man in the pub and everybody had soon joined in, but Ratty's knife had cut the deepest. It was something of a surprise to Jack when he found the stained knife lovingly wrapped in a towel in his father's booze cupboard. He hadn't bothered to dispose it. He was too drunk to care either way.

For years after the grisly discovery, Jack dreamed about the knife, except in those dreams it wasn't his father waving the stained blade — it was him.

The dreams shifted after Seth's murder and in Jack's most recent dreams, he no longer held a knife but a gun instead. In the dreams he pointed the gun at Seth, who didn't seem to care because he knew mere bullets couldn't stop him.

The main difference between Jack and the other tenants at The Cottage was simple; Jack actually rather liked Seth Kevorkian. Jack thought Seth was a bit strange and he was sometimes wary of what he did to people, but Jack also found Seth to be hugely entertaining and tremendously funny. However, not everything Seth did was entertaining to Jack; sometimes Seth's behaviour terrified him…

Jack was bored. Everybody was out at the cinema except for Mother and Seth and Patricia, all of whom remained behind for reasons of their own: Mother was busy, Seth declined, Jack didn't have enough money and Patricia was under sedation. There was nothing on TV and Jack was bored stiff with his Nintendo. He'd completed all the games on his shelf and Lawrence had locked his bedroom door which meant his games were unavailable to Jack.

He was pacing around the halls of The Cottage, wondering what he should do next, when a voice reached his ears. Jack stopped and looked over towards Seth's bedroom door, a frown maturing upon his face. It was definitely Seth's voice, but the word he was shouting over and over again didn't sound like English, in fact it didn't sound like anything Jack had heard in his life.

"Mundara!"

He crept towards Seth's room and gently, tentatively, he pressed his ear against the smooth brown oak paneling of the door…

"Why don't you just come in?" Seth's irritated voice issued from behind the door.

"How did you know I was listening?" Jack said in a mildly wounded tone.

"Do you really think someone with arms the size of tree trunks can sneak about without me hearing? Hurry up and get in here."

Jack looked approvingly at his arms, they were his best feature and he kept them as big as possible. His 'guns' (as he lovingly called them) sometimes got him into trouble. Mother had once sent a group of care workers into his bedroom to search for concealed weapons after she overheard him talking to Lawrence about his 'amazing guns'. She was bewildered and somewhat embarrassed afterwards.

"What are you doing?" Jack asked brashly, his eyes taking in Seth's appearance.

Seth was wearing a crimson robe that gave him the faint air of a Harry Potter fan. He was standing in the middle of his sizeable room, surrounded by candles in a rainbow of different colours and sizes. He didn't look up at Jack; his attention was focused on an ornate chest of drawers with a blood red apple placed on the top.

"I'm trying to cast the Transmat Spell, but it's going nowhere."

Jack could see from the pained expression on Seth's face that he was devastated by his lack of success, and that his own pun was lost on him. Seth pointed his hand in the direction of the apple and shouted:

"Mundara! Mundara! Oh…just move! Mundara!"

But nothing happened apart from the apple wobbling slightly.

"Is this like, you know, magick or something?" Jack couldn't hide his smile.

"Yes!" Seth said in a crestfallen tone. "It's a spell for the transmigration of matter."

"I failed all my exams. Could you rephrase that in English for me?"

Seth dramatically scooped up some crumpled pieces of torn paper from his bed and waved them with hysterical annoyance. Then he walked over to the corner of his room, opened an air vent on the wall, and slipped the paper deep inside.

"In theory I should be able to move that apple using magick. It's supposed to be a simple incantation but I can't get it to work. It's always the simple spells that cause the most trouble. If I can't even perform a simple Transmat enchantment, then I'm a failure, Jack, a real failure."

"You look like a mad monk in that robe," Jack said with a wonky grin.

Seth suddenly burst into peals of gleeful laughter.

"I suppose you're right," he said when he looked down at his costume, "but it feels right. I want to look the part when I finally Conjure The Infinite."

This was the first time Jack remembered hearing Seth use that phrase. Those three little words sounded ominous to Jack, even when spoken aloud by Seth in his silly robe while trying to magickally move an apple. In the coming months Jack would hear those three little words over and over and over again.

'Conjuring The Infinite' was the one thing that preoccupied Seth above all else, the one thing that dominated his way of life and every waking thought.

It was his disgrace. It was his downfall.

"She's never going to go out with me," Jack slurred drunkenly. He had been drinking out of a wine bottle for the last hour, not realising it was empty. If Jack could have seen himself at that exact moment, he would have recoiled from his reflection, because he looked just like his father. Alcohol turned Jack's handsome face upside down, giving him a ratty complexion, but he didn't know this and Seth didn't bother telling him.

The two housemates had ventured outside into the grounds behind The Cottage, close to the edge of the old forest. Seth had produced the bottle of wine, which Jack had thought was strange, because Seth didn't drink alcohol. But that hadn't stopped Jack receiving the bottle gratefully and spending the following hour chatting to Seth about everything and anything.

"My dad's in jail," Jack now said drunkenly.

"Oh!" Seth exclaimed. "Why?"

"He's a murderer."

"My dad is worse than a murderer," Seth said bitterly.

"What's so bad about your dad?" Jack asked.

"He's boring."

"Boring?"

"He *was* boring. He's dead."

A few minutes later, Jack laughed like a loon:

"'What's so bad about your dad?' That rhymes, Seth! It rhymes."

But Seth wasn't listening to Jack any more. Jack stole a glance over at him to see Seth's attention captured by a lone figure standing in the distance. His brain was sluggish from being drowned in alcohol, but Jack still recognised the man, if only because of the smelly brown clothes he was wearing.

It was Soldier Sam. He was waiting to talk to one person and it wasn't Jack.

There was a strange fleeting moment when Jack felt the strength of Seth's disdain for the strange loner. It was almost palpable, but it passed and Seth soon left to go and meet with Sam.

Jack didn't know what they were talking about, but he was too drunk to care, so he sat alone and watched events unfurl before foggy eyes. Random words hovered across the wind towards him, words that his ears caught but didn't form into coherent sentences: "Wife," and "money," and "tell," and "police," and "help" and finally another word Jack would hear again soon…"Bournemouth."

The fight started when Seth slapped Soldier Sam across his face with enough force to rattle poor Sam's head. Even with cheap wine flowing through his veins, Jack could still detect the signs of an impending brawl. He'd seen his own dad do the same thing to innocent people countless times during his childhood. With this very much in mind, Jack leapt up onto his feet and powered towards the weird loner who was being attacked by his housemate.

Jack reached the fight in seconds, his massive arms swinging down on Sam, slamming him onto the grass. But the fight wasn't finished, Jack reached down and pulled Sam up with his hands, then he lifted him right off the ground.

"Kill him!" Seth screamed at Jack, his face red with rage. "Kill him!"

Negative memories from Jack's childhood blurred across his eyes at this exact moment; his father asking him to lie to the police for him, the bloodied knife, all the meals Jack had to cook for himself because his father was too drunk…

"Kill him!" Ratty shouted. "Don't let him disrespect me like that!"

Jack looked at his father's cherry-coloured face and quickly shook his head free of the intoxicating alcohol delusion. It wasn't his father shouting at him, it was Seth.

"Why are you just holding him there? Beat the crap out of him."

Jack released Soldier Sam and did nothing to prevent his getaway.

"You're an idiot Jack," Seth said coldly.

"Why was he here?" Jack's voice was now clear and free of drunkenness.

"He owed me money for help I gave him," Seth said with a slight sneer on his face.

"Soldier Sam owed you money?" Jack was doubtful.

"Yes. He owes me a lot of money and I intend to collect it."

"What did he owe you money for?"

Seth smiled persuasively like he always did when he didn't want to talk any longer.

"Secrets and lies, that kind of thing…"

A CLUE OR TWO
After The Funeral

Jack lied to the others when he told them he needed to go outside for air. He actually wanted to slip away unobserved to Seth's bedroom. Someone else had been in there, and he wanted to know who it was and what they were after.

Whoever it was, Jack thought dourly, they had been interrupted when they heard him and Lawrence climbing the staircase. Since Lawrence had been at his side, Jack knew it wasn't his bald friend, which meant it had to be someone else in The Cottage.

His initial suspicions turned to Mother. Only she had keys to The Abomination's room, and it couldn't have been a coincidence that Patricia had gone on her rampage shortly after he had discovered someone rummaging around Seth's bedroom. But what could Mother possibly want in Seth's room? And why would she deliberately set loose someone to attack her? He just didn't know. Mother wasn't a credible suspect. Jack knew fine well that anyone in The Cottage could have taken the bedroom keys and used them.

The arrival of Campbell Devine was the perfect opportunity for Jack to search Seth's room for himself. Once he got to the door, he cautiously put his hand out, twisting the handle for resistance. It turned first time and Jack smiled happily.

It hasn't been locked yet!

Jack slipped into the darkened room and gently closed the door shut.

The last time Jack was in Seth's room for any real length of time, he had been practicing a spell, seemingly a very simple one, but he couldn't master it. He'd been studying the spell from a stack of print-outs sitting on his bed, indeed Jack remembered Seth fretfully consulting them to try and make sense out of the senseless. Then he…

"What did he do next?" Jack pondered aloud, his memory playing tricks on him. He didn't need to close his eyes to concentrate, because the room was pitch black, so there he stood, casting his mind back to the moment he had walked in on Seth trying to move an apple by mystical means. Seth had been furious and had abandoned the spell. Jack willed his memory to bring the scene back to life again…

(Seth dramatically scooped up some crumpled pieces of torn paper from his bed and waved them with a hysterical annoyance. Then he walked over to the corner of his room, opened the air vent on the wall, and slipped the paper deep inside.)

"He put his notes in the air vent!"

Jack stumbled through the darkness towards the little air vent in the corner of the room, boosted by the idea that if an intruder was looking for something, it would probably be hidden in the hollow space behind the vent.

The vent looked sealed but the screws supporting it were loose enough for Jack to twist with his fingertips. His eyes had become accustomed to the lack of light in the room, so finding the screws on the panel with his fingers wasn't a problem.

What if I find something I don't want to find? Jack thought as the first screw fell away from his fingers. *What if I discover something about Seth I don't want to know? What do I do with the knowledge?*

Seth had certainly changed during the weeks leading up to his death. He had always been slightly distant, thought Jack, even a little bit cold, his interest in magick marking him out as an eccentric. But Jack noticed Seth's personality gradually shifting towards utter malevolence; the defining moment came after the fight with Soldier Sam. That one incident acted like a bucket of icy water thrown over Jack's face, because it allowed him to see that his fellow housemate wasn't just a harmless oddball, he was actually dangerous and manipulative.

Other small incidents made Jack reconsider his modest friendship with Seth: the incident at school with Coryn's diary was particularly spiteful, and the constant verbal jibes Lawrence endured were particularly difficult to ignore. Then there was the mysterious fire at the Community Centre. Although Jack didn't tell anyone, he knew Seth was the cause of that fire, if only because Seth all but admitted it to him a week before his body was discovered on the cliffs.

The second screw came away and the vent dropped onto the carpeted floor.

He didn't know whether the heavy silence was affecting his hearing, or perhaps his imagination was playing tricks on him in the darkness, but Jack thought he could hear voices floating around the room. Old memories absorbed by the walls, waiting for someone to hear them once again, like a brick tape replaying the past.

Maybe Seth's ghost is haunting all of us…

The more Jack thought about it, the more his morbid thought made sense. Wasn't Seth haunting everybody anyway? The memory of him, his deeds, and the events of the funeral were still heavy in Jack's thoughts, and he knew the same was true of everybody else at The Cottage. In a sense, Seth hadn't left them.

Jack thrust his arm into the air vent and felt around the space with his fingers. Something long and round pressed against his fingers, so he rolled it towards him and cautiously lifted it out of the vent.

To Jack's astonishment, he'd discovered what looked like a bullet in the little vent. It didn't take long for him to make the connection between the bullet and Seth's death. He was shot at close range by a mystery gun bearing a mysterious cargo. The implication was clear to Jack.

This is ammunition for a gun. But where is the gun now? Did someone turn Seth's own weapon on him? Where did he get it?

He thoughtfully pocketed the bullet and thrust his arm deeper into the wall. His fingers brushed against more bullets and some loose scraps of paper. He pulled them all gently from the crevice. He pocketed more of the bullets, five of them in total, and then he strained his eyes on the various different print-outs.

They were all typed but some were vandalised with a familiar handwriting which Jack recognised as Seth's. His handwriting was schizophrenic: some of his letters were written in capitals and others written in lower case, usually in the same word. They reflected the mind of the writer.

The heading on the top page read:

How to Conjure the Infinite!

The rest of the sheet was filled with smartly typed words in a language Jack didn't comprehend, but he knew it was the same spell Seth had attempted on Halloween. His eyes soon wandered over towards hastily scribbled schizophrenic handwriting.

The wrong spell but did she do it on purpose? That would

explain the birds.

Jack could almost feel the frustration in Seth's pen as he had scribbled the note. He had evidently marked the page with a large cross so he wouldn't use it in the future.

Tensing his eyes to read the next bits of paper, Jack decided it wasn't worth the bother, so he put the sheets inside his hoodie and crept out of the room. He suddenly exhaled a loud gust of breath when he crossed Seth's door back out into the hallway. He hadn't realised how oppressive the room had been for him.

It only took Jack a few minutes to hide Seth's notes in his own room. He chose underneath his bed as the best hiding place. Jack's rancid socks, baseball bat and samurai sword bought for twenty quid were there and nobody would go near them.

He would return and read the rest of the notes at bedtime.

Ten minutes passed before someone slipped back into Seth's room and found the discarded vent sitting on the floor where Jack had left it. Their first attempt at searching Seth's room had been unsuccessful because of Jack and Lawrence, but now there was a new problem. The intruder, who didn't have much time, quickly realised that the vent had been a hiding place all along. Someone else had found potentially incriminating notes and they could ruin everything.

The prowler exited Seth's room full of disappointment and headed back downstairs to rejoin the others.

DOWN THE PLUG HOLE/ ROUND THE BEND
After The Funeral

"I'm going for a bath," Reet announced suddenly.

"Can I walk you to your door?" Lawrence said hopefully.

"No!" Reet snapped at him. As much as she liked Lawrence (and she did a lot) she was tired of all the attention he continually lavished upon her. He laughed at her jokes even when she knew they weren't funny, he followed her around The Cottage with patient persistence, he fought on her behalf no matter what and yet she didn't feel impressed by his dedication. In fact she found it utterly draining.

"It's been a long day," Reet said emotionlessly, "I just want to have a bath and relax. I might come back downstairs once I've washed my hair."

Lawrence decided to try another tactic in his never-ending bid to impress Reet:

"Do you want me to stand outside your door? Just incase Patricia comes back?"

This tactic, however, crashed and burned in the most humiliating way.

"I think I'll be safe in my room," Reet said dryly.

Lawrence knew when he'd been shot down, so he didn't say anything else. Instead he turned away and faced the fireplace, his face illuminated by the fiery depths of the hearth. He looked so hurt that Reet felt her heart overflowing with pity for him.

"Don't worry about it, baldy," Reet said with a smile. "I'll be back down soon."

Lily looked sharply over at Reet with curious eyes, a strange expression playing over her face, but she couldn't quite put her uneasiness into words. Her eyes followed Reet as she headed towards the grand hallway and the stairs.

Reet was midway up the staircase as Coryn journeyed down. The two girls ignored each other.

As much as Reet adored animals, there was genus of creatures that she couldn't bear whatsoever. Tiny little creatures that reduced her to a spasm of fear which always manifested itself as a dreadful scream: spiders. Big spiders or small spiders; eight legs, patient and crawling; silent and creepy spiders.

The reason for this arachnophobia was an incident which stemmed back to her early childhood. Her older sister, a fiend, was to blame because she had forced Reet to pick up the spider in the bathtub. Because of this memory, Reet's first action upon entering a bathroom was to shout down the plug hole, just to check there were no secret spiders hiding in the darkness.

It was one of Reet's more colourful habits but the only way she could take a bath or a shower was to shout at the plug hole, a technique taught to her by Mother. Reet's peculiar bathtime ritual had its drawbacks though. It was something Seth found endlessly amusing, another weapon in his grand arsenal of bitchy comments.

Reet pulled the chain on the ceiling and her bathroom was bathed in bright, brash, uncontaminated light. Her personal bathroom was tiled black and white; it looked good when exposed to bright light. Reet could spend nearly an hour in a roasting hot bath, relaxing her body from all the stresses and strains of her life. She kept her medication in her bathroom along with a big bottle of bug killer.

She cautiously leaned forward to shout into the plug hole. Every now and then, Reet would have a nasty fantasy that a giant spider would leap out of the plug and attach itself to her face, but Mother told her that such things were impossible.

"Itsy bitsy spider went up the water spout..." Reet's voice wavered as it called down into the depths of the plug hole. She waited and watched to see if her echoing voice would drive out any tiny intruders.

ITSY BITSY SPIDER WENT UP THE WATER SPOUT! SPOUT! SPOUT! SPOUT!

No spider crawled out of the plug hole and Reet suddenly felt a massive weight lift off her ribcage. She breathed a huge sigh of relief and reached out to the ornate silver tap marked with a red circle. Her hand barely touched the tap before she heard an ominous rumbling from deep inside the dark plug hole.

Something sloshed inside the bottomless pipes.

Reet leaned over the tub and peered into the hole with one eye.

An echo floated up, spreading itself outwards from the depths of the drain.

"*Reet...*" a wary voice moaned.

Reet pulled away from the bathtub and uttered a scream of terror, before falling onto the laminate floor and rolling fearfully towards the tiled walls. It wasn't just the fact she'd heard a voice coming out of the plug hole that frightened her, it was the realisation that she recognised the voice, that unbearably familiar voice.

"Reet..." Seth Kevorkian called out from nowhere and everywhere.

"What do you want?" Reet cried out.

"They will...never find me here...the deal is broken...the pact is over..."

Reet's heart pounded with an almost fatal intensity. The sound of her heartbeat was louder than Seth's voice such was the intensity of her fright. Then a strange kind of calmness took hold of her and she listened intently to Seth's words.

"...will fail... cannot conjure the power...I am here now..."

"Where are you?" Reet's voice was low but Seth seemed to hear her regardless.

There was nothing but the sound of a heart beating and gurgling from pipes.

"Are you dead?"

"They will arrive...shortly...I know they will..."

"Who will?"

(Beatbeatbeatbeatbeatbeatbeatbeat)

"They are...coming...won't find me...here..."

Reet didn't quite understand the meaning behind Seth's words.

Suddenly the bathroom filled with demonic laughter, she could feel it in her ears, overwhelming her hearing, so loud it savagely cut into her brain. Reet screamed and slammed her hands into her ears in an attempt to block Seth's mocking laughter, but she couldn't stop the echo inside her head.

Her throat was hoarse with screaming and suddenly her voice gave out into painful peace.

Lawrence dramatically burst through the door and into the bathroom, his face turning in all directions until he found Reet. She was writhing on the floor, apparently in pain from some sort of silent assault. Lawrence fell onto his knees, his arms wrapped lovingly around her until she stopped her secret soundless screaming.

"It was Seth!" Reet shrieked hysterically once her voice returned. "I swear it was!"

When Reet looked up at the bathroom mirror, Seth waved back at her mockingly.

SORCERY, LIES, AND VIDEOGAMES

What started off as a fun trip to the local Community Centre rapidly degenerated into a nightmare. Seth, however, wasn't entirely to blame for this incident.

It was Coryn who first heard about the new-fangled Community Centre. She burst into The Cottage dining room, sweaty with effort, raving about the rumoured new music studio which had been set up inside the Centre using government money.

The aim of the studio, according to what Coryn had been told, was to give the dispossessed teenagers of The Village a chance to show off their musical skills, thus keeping them off the streets. It was a pilot scheme which had been picked up by other towns swamped with teenage gang crime. Coryn couldn't actually sing but made up for her lack of talent with heaps of helpful delusion.

"I've heard about it," Reet said with a flick of her pixie hairstyle. "The Animal Welfare Society have started meeting in the new Centre. They get free cups of tea and chocolate digestives! I've been dying to get inside that place. I might see Lloyd."

(An edgy silence descended upon the others, but Reet didn't

seem to notice.)

Seth broke the silence by dropping his cutlery. He exclaimed gleefully:

"We must go tomorrow! Are any of you in session?"

"I am," Lawrence stated in a dismal tone. "Lily is probing my past. She believes my traumatic upbringing is the source of my problems."

"I don't know why we have to put up with her idiosyncrasies. I wouldn't trust her as far as I could kick her, baldy," Seth ranted at the mention of Lily's name. "Let's all take a trip to The Community Centre! I've heard they've got the new Okama Gamesphere III and I *have* to see it in action."

Despite Lawrence's detestation of Seth, he soon found himself agreeing to his demand. Seth could be very persuasive when he wanted to do something. This was Seth at his finest, leading the others instead of persecuting them, taking them on one of his crusades. His fixations were constantly in flux but Seth always remained determined, motivated, and somehow inspirational.

The next morning was an eventful one. A small exploration party from The Cottage ventured out towards The Community Centre. They were full of barely contained excitement. This group consisted of Seth, Coryn, Lawrence and Reet. Jack couldn't come because his probation officer was paying him a visit, while Julee couldn't join the others because she had to visit Teen Alcoholics Anonymous.

"I've got so much to tell The Animal Welfare Society!" Reet chanted.

Coryn, however, was the happiest out of all of them.

"I can't wait to record a song. I might even send it to a record company."

Seth looked over at Coryn as he walked down the road away from The Cottage.

"You'd have to lose a lot of weight. Record companies don't sign fatties."

"I'll knock you out!" Coryn shouted angrily.

The little group laughed like they always did when Coryn threw a temper tantrum.

Mrs. Celia Grossman hated the noise generated by the toddler reading group. She didn't see the point in mothers pretending to themselves that their toddlers could read; after all, baby brains were too underdeveloped to understand story narrative.

Celia suspected the misplaced enthusiasm was really for the parents themselves. It was so they could show off to their friends about just how smart their offspring were because they had a meaningless certificate on the wall of the nursery.

"Oh my baby is so smart!" These annoying parents probably boasted over cappuccinos. "He loves books so much! He's even got the certificate to prove it."

Mrs. Celia Grossman also hated the teenagers who visited the Centre just so they could play video games. She ached to walk over and tell them to get jobs.

However, if Celia Grossman hated something more than teenagers playing video games, it was the teenagers living at The Cottage. She had been forced to desecrate the Community Centre walls with posters bearing the slogan, *Just Because I Live in Care, It Doesn't Mean You Shouldn't Care About Me.* She resented the posters and their insidious propaganda, because she knew the truth about people at The Cottage. The faces changed over the years, but the tenants all had one thing in common: Each and every one of them was trouble! They were the bastard offspring of drunks, druggies, dole scum, and immigrants. Celia loathed them all. She particularly despised Mother's tireless attempts at rehabilitating these terrible teens. In Celia's opinion, criminals and their children did not deserve to be helped! She felt they needed a firm hand, a commanding voice, a good kick up the...

A harsh voice derailed Celia's train of thought.

"Hello! Can you hear me? Hello! WHY AREN'T YOU LISTENING?"

The teenage boy had the most piercing blue eyes Celia had ever seen in her life. His curly hair was in need of a good cut and his mouth was inverted into a yellow smile.

"I think the old dingbat is deaf," the insolent teenager said to his friends.

"How dare you!" Celia gurgled. "What do you want?"

"We've come to visit the recently refurbished Community Centre and avail ourselves of your facilities and the new Okama Gamesphere."

Celia felt her face drop into an expression of severe disappointment, but things were about to get much worse for Mrs. Grossman.

The teenage brat's voice, when he spoke again, was laced with noxious sarcasm that Celia simply did not appreciate. He also had an unattractive habit of rolling his eyes.

"We've come all the way from The Cottage," the brat said. "Let us in!"

Although she didn't know it, Celia Grossman had just been introduced to Seth Kevorkian.

The previous Community Centre had fallen into such a state of disrepair that legendary stories had started up about the place. One of the best was a tall tale about two pensioners having afternoon tea in the café, only to find their chat interrupted by the sound of the nearby wall collapsing into dust.

Except that wasn't a tall tale, it really did happen.

Mrs. Celia Grossman was instrumental in the campaign to get a new and improved Community Centre built on the same grounds as the old building. She got her wish and was installed as official caretaker by the governing committee. Celia swelled with pride when she won the job until she was informed that, as part of her job, she would have to target The Three Ts which made up the Centre's main audience.

The Three Ts wasn't the official name for the three main types of people wanted by the commission; it was Celia's secret name for them, a shortened version of 'Teens, Tramps and Toddlers'. The three worst groups of people in the world! The toddler crowd was already full of overweight young mothers with spotty boyfriends barely out of school. Those people were only good for creating junky babies and sponging off the government. The Community Centre was too good for them!

"Why can't the pensioners come back?" Celia wondered with genuine despair.

Over the following weeks Celia developed an obsession with ridding the Community Centre of the scum from The Cottage. They were worse than The Three Ts in many ways because they were a union of the first two Ts (Teens and Tramps) gone disgustingly wrong. Celia knew this was what happened when bad parents decided to procreate. Sometimes, in her lowest moments, Celia wished she could have children, because she knew they wouldn't be anything like that awful Cottage lot. But she cheered herself up with the thought that her work in the Community Centre was all-consuming and left little time for a family.

It was during one of her low periods that Celia finally concocted a plan to rid the Community Centre of the invading delinquent brats and reclaim it for herself.

Celia waited until the fat girl from The Cottage booked a session in the mini recording studio before she acted out her scheme. The studio technician, a gangly young man with a horrific range of ties, worked there on a voluntary basis. He considered the time spent helping teenagers record noisy songs completely worthwhile; he especially loved telling the teenagers about the time his band supported the Arctic Monkeys. Celia must have heard that story a dozen times now.

One day when he left the studio, a few minutes before the fat girl from The Cottage entered for her recording time, Celia crept in with a large cup of Coca-Cola clasped firmly in her trembling hands. She'd observed the fat girl drinking Diet Coke (that made Celia laugh) so it made sense to use that brand of drink for her secret mission.

Celia wavered at first, suddenly pinned down by an attack on her conscience, but she reasoned this was for the best. If she allowed the scum from The Cottage to infest the lovely new Community Centre, they would ruin it with crime and thievery.

With that thought in mind, Mrs. Celia Grossman carried out the rest of her plan.

She tipped the full cup of Diet Coke over the mixing board of the recording studio.

She didn't stay to witness the result of her handiwork; she only needed to hear the fizzing sparks to know she'd damaged the studio equipment beyond repair. A real shame, thought Celia as she fled the little booth, because it was all brand new.

Now all she had to do was throw blame onto the big girl from The Cottage. That wouldn't be difficult, Celia thought smugly to herself, because everyone would automatically blame someone from The Cottage anyway.

Seth didn't take too kindly to being expelled from the Community Centre.

"Why am I getting banned?" he said without once taking his eyes off the Okama Gamesphere. "Why don't you just ban that daft cow? She made the mess, not me!"

Celia was rather shocked by his lack of loyalty for a fellow housemate. His punishing words emboldened Celia's resolve; she quickly decided to remove this dreadful boy from the premises no matter what happened in the process. Decisive action was required! With that in mind, Celia shot past Seth and tore the Okama Gamesphere plug out of the wall, instantly killing off the power to Seth's video game.

It took him a few seconds to realise what Celia had done.

"You withered up old dog!" Seth screamed in vibrato. "I curse you! I curse you forever! You will feel the full fury of The Infinite. I mean it! I will become all-powerful! I shall erase you from existence. You've ruined my game…Ohhhhh."

"You can use your magick powers to get yourself a new Okama Gamesphere," Celia said with a laugh as burly security guards tossed Seth out onto the street.

Time passed slowly but Celia allowed herself to take a deep breath, gently savouring the silence as a result of her hard earned victory.

Someone set fire to the Community Centre two days later. By the time Celia arrived at the scene, she was dismayed to see the new building had disappeared, a blackened husk in its place. The fire engines were almost empty and the fires still blazed audaciously as firemen tried vainly to quell the inferno.

Celia couldn't bear to watch her beautiful Community Centre ablaze, so she turned away from the flames only to be confronted by a figure in the near distance. She felt the heat from the fire but also a different kind of heat, the heat caused by anger and frustration. She had been defeated by a superior foe.

Seth Kevorkian winked at Celia before disappearing into the gloomy forest.

FROG VERSUS TOAD
After The Funeral

"Didn't you predict freak weather conditions when you arrived earlier tonight?" Coryn asked in a voice menaced by panic.

Campbell looked over at Coryn and waggled his eyebrows in her direction. She was right, he had indeed predicted freak weather conditions earlier, a forecast taken from a story he'd read in a newspaper that had yet to been written.

"Oh yes, I did." Campbell was now on his fourth cup of tea as he waited patiently for something to happen. People were wandering in and out of the living room and it was difficult for him to remember their names. The only time he effectively recalled names was if they belonged to paying customers.

"I think you're right. Something very weird is going on outside!"

Campbell stood up and idly wandered over to the window Coryn was standing alongside. He wasn't alone; Lily entered the living room, accompanied by Jack, Lawrence and Reet. It seemed Reet had given up on having a bath, but a quick glance at her revealed a shaken and upset girl. Coryn's twitchy reaction to the weather outside wasn't helping settle Reet's nervousness.

Julee pressed her face against the window so she could see what was causing all the fuss. Something fell and bounced against the pane of glass with a loud SPLAT. It happened again, and again. She was the first to scream when she realised the cause. It was her reaction which set off Coryn, who leapt away from the window, finally convinced about the fear factor from outside. Lily didn't scream, nor did she flinch from the bizarre sight outside, but she was slightly unnerved. She watched over the odd weather with a detached methodical curiosity.

"Is that what I think it is?" Lawrence said hoarsely.

"If you think its raining frogs," Jack replied, "then yes it is!"

"I knew it." Julee tried to calm herself down. "But I didn't believe it."

"Freak weather conditions?" Jack said. "Frogs are falling down from the sky!"

Campbell placed the empty cup in his hands down on a nearby lamp stand. He looked over at Jack and corrected him, "Those aren't frogs outside."

Jack relaxed somewhat, but he didn't stay calm for long.

"Those are toads." Campbell's eyes twitched. "They're *much* slimier."

"Oh great," Jack yelled, "I'm really pleased you know the difference."

The rain was thundering down on The Cottage, except it wasn't water, it was a rain of toad. Hundreds of the little green slimy creatures bounced off the pavement and the roof, leaping and croaking with surprise at their new surroundings. Some detonated against the window, causing the housemates to recoil in disgust as green goo sprayed outside of the panes.

"Tomorrow's newspapers will suggest that what we're seeing…"

Lily scornfully interrupted Campbell before he could finish his sentence.

"Oh here we go again!"

"As I was saying," Campbell said between narrow eyes, "tomorrow's newspapers will suggest that what we're seeing is the result of a random typhoon from India."

Nobody in the room uttered a sound. They looked at each other in various expressions of bafflement. Their day had started off with a funeral and it had been plunged into a night of twists and turns so bizarre that nobody could have invented them.

"A typhoon from India?" Julee said in a deadpan voice.

The sounds caused by the rain of toad started to subside.

"It's just like Halloween," Reet said quietly, "with all those birds."

"A typhoon from India? I mean…really?" Julee repeated.

Campbell looked around for a cup of tea but found nothing. He looked pleadingly towards Julee who in turn nudged Jack. Without saying a word, Jack understood and undertook his tea-making mission, leaving the room to carry it out.

"That's what the newspapers think," Campbell replied with a shrug of his shoulders.

Lily decided the best way to proceed here was to humour the madman.

"What is the truth? Can your powers tell us where the toads have come from?"

Campbell didn't answer until Jack returned with another cup of tea, which the psychic received most gratefully. Lily considered the idea that Campbell could graduate into a show business career, because everything he did was overdramatic, all the way down to how he drank his tea. But when he spoke, his face was grave.

"Seth came to visit me in my shop a few days before he died.

When I looked at his face, I felt the weight of destiny bearing down upon him. And there was something else, something unearthly…three shadowy figures stood behind him."

Mention of 'three shadowy figures' drew out a gasp of fear from Reet.

Lily opened her mouth to reply, but she decided not to bother saying anything. Campbell continued talking as he always did, steering the conversation towards what exactly was causing the freak weather conditions.

"You don't need psychic powers to know that Seth was on a mission. Those three things from my psychic examination were Seth's future, emissaries of a creature that has no right to exist in the rational world. Seth has since contacted The Infinite. I felt it reach into this dimension, I nearly fainted because of the psychic whiplash."

Campbell paused to drink some tea and allow the housemates to process his words. Coryn looked scared. Jack and Lawrence didn't show any reaction. Julee and Lily wore expressions of fascination while Reet seemed slightly distant.

When Campbell spoke again, his voice cooled the atmosphere in the warm room, and suddenly the housemates couldn't feel the heat of the fireplace on their backs.

"The day I felt The Infinite reach into this world was the same day Seth Kevorkian was shot on the cliffs. The weird weather is a side effect of a very powerful enchantment gone wrong. The laws of physics, probability, and natural order are being usurped. Something nasty is coming to The Cottage."

Campbell had no sooner finished speaking when the lights went out.

READER, I DID NOT MARRY HIM

Dear Diary, Coryn wrote with a chewed-up pen, *I know that today is going to be a good day, because Derek Sullivan is going to ask me out and my Dad asked my Mum out when she was fifteen and they fell in love and got married and had me. Or maybe they had me and then got married. I think Derek would be a good boyfriend but he would be an even better husband!*

Coryn laughed and fell about her bed. It was the kind of laughter that rocked her body, because it came from a place of joy. Her diary was full of these kinds of fantasies and secrets. It wasn't so much a diary; it was more an unpublished teen romance novel starring Coryn and whatever boy she currently had a crush on. But Coryn liked writing down her dreams so she could re-read and relive them. Reality was dull because there wasn't any background music and the boys she liked usually preferred Julee. Only Coryn knew that Derek didn't actually exist. His name was code for the real object of Coryn's affections. Whenever she wrote down the word 'Derek', she was actually thinking about Jack.

"What are you writing in that stupid diary now?"

An infuriatingly familiar voice gleefully interrupted Coryn's early morning diary update. She instinctively pushed her diary and old pen underneath her bed covers.

"I'm not writing anything." Coryn tried forcing a smile at the newest arrival at The Cottage. It was more difficult than she anticipated. The sight of Seth's sarcastic face made it difficult for Coryn to smile. She couldn't even fake it. Her facial muscles contracted into a grimace before she could do anything to prevent it.

Seth ignored Coryn's comment. "I'd like to read it one day. I think it would be an interesting experience. Why don't you let everybody see it?"

Seth's suggestion sent a surge of electrical terror through Coryn. She would rather go out and swallow a bolt of lightning than give Seth free access to her dreams. The last thing she wanted was for strangers to see the contents of her diary, because even if Jack's name wasn't explicit in it, people might still be able to guess the real identity of 'Derek'. It was clearly Coryn's turn to be victimized by Seth. He chose his victims at random, depending on his mood. In the short time since he had arrived at The Cottage, he'd done everything in his power to make the lives of his fellow housemates a living hell.

Seth had a real genius for tormenting people and getting away with it.

"It's not a diary," Coryn said smoothly. "It's just a book I scribble notes in."

"Is it a story?" Seth asked sweetly.

"Yes!" Coryn grabbed at his suggestion, but she had a horrible feeling that he was toying with her, that he already knew what was inside her diary.

There's no way he could have read it. I would know! Coryn thought.

Seth continued pushing for information.

"Is it based on your life?"

"Why are you so bloody nosy? It's all just stuff I made up. Okay?"

The peculiar smile never left Seth's face. He stood absolutely motionless, vigilantly studying Coryn's face, his eyes absorbing even the smallest bit of discomfiture.

Then Seth opened his mouth and unleashed a torrent of abuse that effortlessly demolished the remaining fragments of Coryn's self-esteem.

"Is your book about a fat chick called Coryn who can't get a boyfriend? Why can't you get a boyfriend? Why can't you be more like Julee? Jack would fancy you if you were like Julee. But you're nothing like Julee, isn't that right Coryn?"

"Screw you! Why are you so horrible to people?" Coryn screamed. There was nothing more she could say after that. Words seemed to bounce right off Seth Kevorkian. Nothing had any effect on him. She couldn't even beat him up, because he'd just fetch The Abomination and it would be game over. But Coryn really, desperately wanted to batter Seth. She wanted to do a Riverdance on his face and gouge his eyes out. She hated him so much! She wanted to kill him.

Seth giggled one last time, then he left Coryn's bedroom. But the emotional sting caused by his remarks took longer to depart. Coryn waited and wiped her eyes. Then she cried into her hands for a few minutes. After she'd finished emptying her eyes, she drew herself a bath and soaked in silence for ten minutes.

Coryn's final act before leaving for school was to make sure her diary was safely tucked away. She'd been warned by Lily that Seth had a thing about other people's diaries, and she didn't want him snooping on all of her secrets.

Coryn wasn't a traditional beauty by any means. From her mother she inherited tangled hair and low self-esteem. From her father she inherited a flushed complexion and various mental illnesses. Coryn constantly despaired at her lot in life. She knew she wasn't the smartest girl, she sometimes got jealous of other girls, but Coryn prided herself on being fun and loyal to her real friends. The problem was that she had no real friends. The girls in The Cottage weren't actually friends, but glorified flatmates, and her parents were long gone in a haze of booze and arguments.

At school (just like at The Cottage) Coryn simply existed; not hugely popular but not totally unpopular. She fell sharply into the middle of the school hierarchy. There was nothing special about her in any way. She was The Fat Girl from The Cottage.

Seth, however, seemed to cast a spell over anybody he met. His looks, his personality and charisma seemed to reach out and stun everyone in his orbit. Coryn had tried in vain to work out Seth's secret. She wanted to try and tap into a little bit of his power, to siphon off some of his glamour, but she couldn't do it.

Sometimes, from a safe distance in the school grounds, Coryn would stand and watch him attentively. She wanted to see what he did to make all these friends, what he said to reduce people to slavish servants of his cult. Coryn wanted people to tell her that she was cool, that she was funny, and that she wasn't a loony.

People seemed to forget Seth also lived up at The Cottage, just like her.

But try as she might, Coryn could never work out the secret of Seth's success. There were times when Seth spoke to people in an agreeable voice only to transform into a snarling horror once they'd left his presence:

"I'll see you in class, Seth. I'll save you a seat!"

"I can't wait, Laura! It should be a laugh."

Then,

"Save me a pair of ear plugs too, Laura, so I can ignore your horsey voice."

Coryn would try and join in on the bitching, but Seth would ignore her contributions. She wasn't even good enough to join in the banter with him.

"Have you seen Laura's legs? They look like she's rubbed a Brillo pad up them for hours. Oh don't look at me like that! I say the stuff people are afraid to say."

Coryn remembered that comment, it made her silently vow to start being as outspoken as Seth. Coryn wanted to say the stuff people were afraid to say; she wanted that kind of confidence more than anything in the world.

She wanted the power to turn the unreal events of her diary into her real life.

The housemates were waiting patiently for Coryn at the bottom of the staircase in the hall. As Coryn approached them, she felt the hurtling weight of Seth displacing the air. He effortlessly passed her, such was his speed. His timing was odd, because when Coryn walked by Seth's bedroom on the way to the stairs, she could have sworn Seth was running himself a bath. Surely he couldn't have washed, dried and put his clothes on *that* quickly?

Seth was gone by the time everybody ventured out of The Cottage for school.

"Have a productive day!" Mother called out from her office window.

Julee stuck her tongue out when Mother turned away, a silly gesture of defiance.

Coryn laughed at Julee's blatant insolence, but then a queer jealousy took hold of her, as it always did whenever Julee did something everybody liked. Mother assured her that these feelings of inadequacy could be beaten, that she didn't have to be jealous of anyone. Coryn didn't believe Mother. The intensity of the resentment she felt towards people was frightening to Coryn, yet strangely comforting.

"I wonder where Seth is off to in such a hurry," Julee said, her eyes straining to see him running off into the distance.

"I was thinking the exact same thing," Coryn replied.

"He's probably off to meet one of his friends at school," Jack said with a shrug.

"He'll probably take their lunch money too," Julee muttered.

The subject was changed and Coryn quickly forgot about Seth's strange behaviour.

"So your propensity for lying extends to your diary entries?"

Coryn nodded in agreement with Lily's assessment.

"Diaries are there for us to note down our thoughts, to set out the events of our lives, the day to day details and patterns that bind them. Lying to your diary, it could be argued, is like lying to yourself. It is a very unusual thing to do with a diary."

Coryn nodded in agreement with Lily's assessment.

"One day, that kind of behaviour could get you into a lot of trouble."

Coryn nodded in agreement with Lily's assessment.

"I have a diary too," Lily said softly, "I put everything inside it, all of my most private thoughts and ideas. I can't imagine what would happen if someone stole it. I imagine it would be awful. It would be like someone reading my soul."

Coryn nodded in agreement with Lily's assessment.

Coryn didn't realise anything was wrong until her second lesson which, incidentally, also happened to be her least favourite in the world. Mathematics was boring and she couldn't count, so it was a waste of time her being there. The class was headed by Mr. Wardle, who looked and smelled like a dirty biker. Mr. Wardle seemed to think that the best way to teach his pupils was to wear a hoodie and pepper his conversations with the word 'dude'.

There Coryn sat, her eyes swimming away from the white board, going under with sublime tiredness...until the giggling started. She suddenly became aware of people in the classroom glancing and pointing at her. It was the strangest sight to witness because nobody ever paid her any attention.

Then it became apparent they knew something that she didn't.

"What is it?" Coryn said loudly. "What are you all staring at?"

The bell for recess trilled and Coryn used it to make a mercy escape somewhere private; anywhere she would be left alone, far away from prying eyes and nasty whispers. But the laughter and whispering followed her no matter where she went.

"WHAT ARE YOU POINTING AT?!" Coryn raged at a first year pupil, a small girl with chestnut hair, who stopped in the middle of a corridor to point at her.

But the girl wasn't pointing at Coryn. She was pointing at something behind Coryn. Slowly, very slowly, Coryn turned to see what was holding the first year's interest. A crowd was standing behind Coryn, looking at what appeared to be bits of paper stapled to the school notice board.

The handwriting on the sheets of paper looked horribly familiar.

"Oh no," Coryn croaked. "This can't be happening."

It was her secret diary, except it was no longer a secret. Everybody was reading it.

Dear Diary, I know that today is going to be a good day, because Jack From The Cottage is going to ask me out...

Coryn noticed the name 'Derek Sullivan' had been scrubbed out of her diary entries and replaced with the words 'Jack from The Cottage'. She quickly became aware of a large cheaply-made sign above the notice board which screamed out:

CORYN'S PATHETIC LIFE (Or 'Why Doesn't Jack Fancy Me?')

"That's not my diary!" Coryn babbled at everybody. "I swear it isn't my diary!"

"But it looks like your handwriting," a voice said calmly from behind her, "and there's no-one else at this school called 'Coryn'."

Coryn spun around to see Seth standing against the wall. She felt her chest tighten and her hands contract into heavy fists. It wouldn't take much to smash Seth's face into a pulp. She wanted to do it. She'd be doing the world a favour.

"I hate myself because I'm so fat and Jack fancies Julee..."

Coryn stopped as the unfamiliar words reached her. The chestnut-haired girl, the same one who had pointed the notice board out to Coryn, was reciting the diary entries loudly so people at the back of the crowd could hear her. There was only one problem with these particular diary entries...

"I didn't write that," Coryn said, "I know I didn't write that!"

This time she was actually telling the truth.

"I thought it would be funny to change some of the

entries in your diary," Seth sniggered at her, "and faking your underdeveloped handwriting wasn't too difficult, it was like copying the scribbling of a manic infant. Now I've added whole chapters into your diary that improves the quality of the piece. You can thank me later."

Coryn seethed. She could barely move for her anger but she felt utterly helpless.

"You want me to thank you? I'm going to kick your head in!"

Seth shrugged nonchalantly.

"I think I'd start apologising to everybody first."

"Why?" Coryn snarled.

"I've written a whole page on how much you hate Teresa McGinley and her friends. Some of the descriptions I've used are utterly vile!"

Seth had chosen his targets well. Teresa McGinley was the supreme bitch of a particularly vicious gang operating at school. If she or any of her posse had read Seth's faked diary entries, they would want to beat her up. If Coryn got into one fight at school, she might get kicked out of The Cottage and sent back home to live with her father, the man she despised more than anyone in the world. Well, with the exception of Seth Kevorkian.

"You're an evil little..."

Seth waved a finger mockingly at Coryn.

"I'm not evil," he laughed, "but with practice I might improve."

"I asked you a question this morning," Coryn said with her head held high, "and I want you to answer it. Right here, Seth, right now. I want an answer."

Seth looked blankly at her.

"Why are you so horrible to people?" Coryn reminded him.

"I don't know," he replied with absolute sincerity, "there's something in me Coryn...I can't help it...I've tried to be better and bigger...but no matter what I do, I don't feel satisfied or happy. Nothing I do can ever make me happy except..."

"Except gaining the approval of The Infinite," Coryn said sarcastically.

"Yes," whispered Seth, his eyes staring past Coryn into another dimension.

"So this is all meaningless!" Coryn cried out. "There *is* no Infinite. It's all crap!"

The bell for third class ended the argument, but it seemed to have little effect of the growing crowd of pupils reading the pieces of paper stuck to the wall. They were all laughing at the flowery prose and the venomous attacks on well-known classmates. Coryn wanted to scream at them, to let them know it was Seth who had written the nasty stuff, but deep down she knew they wouldn't believe her.

Seth, in writing all that bile, had put onto paper how Coryn truly felt about people around her. That, more than anything, made her feel ashamed.

Mother didn't take news of Coryn's suspension lightly. Mr. Taylor, the headmaster at school, had no choice but to suspend her for a week. He was particularly saddened at the horrible things Coryn had written about him.

It later transpired that Seth had composed a particularly gross epitaph about the headmaster in an exact copy of Coryn's own writing. Mr. Taylor didn't believe Coryn's protestations of innocence, nor did he believe that Seth would ever steal her diary. The final insult came when the headmaster told Coryn she should follow Seth's example and treat people with 'kindness and respect'.

Like most adults, Mr. Taylor couldn't see beyond Seth's glittery personality.

Coryn would never discover the motives behind Seth's malicious actions that day. By the time she mustered up the confidence to confront him, it was already too late.

Someone else got there first and shot him dead on a midwinter afternoon.

DELIVERANCE AND BELLIGERENCE
After The Funeral

"What's happening?" Reet's voice shrieked.

"It's just a power cut," Lily snapped at her. She was beginning to tire of the housemates and their histrionics. Having to constantly reassure them of their safety had become tiresome. But the uneasy feeling coming from the pit of her stomach wouldn't disappear. She felt sick as thoughts of Campbell's prediction played and replayed themselves in her head: Someone was going to leave The Cottage and never return. *Someone was going to leave The Cottage and never return. Someone was going to leave The Cottage and never return.* Lily didn't know what would make anyone leave The Cottage, but the silly psychic had been absolutely correct in his predictions thus far. The freak weather conditions he spoke of had manifested as a rain of toad! An impossibility and yet she watched it happen with her own eyes. Not for the first time that night Lily wondered just how much Campbell knew about Seth's murder. She needed to know the truth so she could finally put this mess into the past where it belonged.

"I'm scared!" Reet called out. Lawrence rushed over and stood protectively beside her. He would have looked more macho if he hadn't tripped over a footstool in the darkness, but Reet appreciated the concern anyway.

"It's only a busted fuse," Julee said, fully aware that she didn't sound convincing to herself let alone her friend.

"Are you scared Lloyd is coming for you?" Coryn's voice said nastily in the dark.

"I haven't seen Lloyd since The Steak Place," Reet retorted, but she didn't sound confident.

The mention of Lloyd's name gave Lily authorisation to enquire whether or not Reet had been taking her regular dosage of pills. Normally she wouldn't discuss individual cases in front of the other housemates, but they were all trapped in the house in complete darkness, utterly terrified. Lily wanted to know if she was safe from Reet's vengeful persona, the same personality that had convinced her to break into a meat packing factory and free all the cows. Reet called him Lloyd and she honestly believed him to be real. Lily's sessions couldn't convince her otherwise.

Lloyd *wasn't* real though. Lloyd only existed inside Reet's head.

"If you keep taking your medication, Lloyd won't come back. He isn't real. He's a manifestation of your multiple personality disorder. Resist the illusion."

When Reet spoke, her voice was much steadier, more controlled, almost angry:

"I haven't seen Lloyd. He isn't coming back. OK?"

Lawrence opened his mouth to say something, but a crushing glare from Reet stopped the words before they could tumble out. He didn't know if he should speak about what had happened in Reet's bathroom. She was utterly convinced that Seth had been talking to her through the pipes running underneath her bathtub. However, it didn't take long for something else to distract him from his own thoughts.

A powerful torchlight beam cut through the darkness. It momentarily dazzled the others, but soon they found the source of the light in the hands of Campbell Devine.

"I predicted the lights would go off, so I brought a torch with me."

"How do we know you didn't rig the power to go off?" Lily snarled.

"You don't, my dear, you don't." Campbell said with a slight glint of menace in his darkened eyes. "Now how about you go and fix the lights."

Lily stormed off, but her annoyance was observable even in darkness.

"I believe you," Julee said, "I believe your powers are for real."

The admission surprised Campbell. He remembered his first meeting with Julee when Reet brought her into his shop for a reading. It hadn't gone well at all.

"Last time we met, you thought I was an oddball. What's changed?"

Julee thought about the best way to explain her sudden change of opinion, but she didn't want to sound like a candidate for Castlekrankie Mental Hospital — where Patricia would probably end her days. So she edited her recent experiences in The Tronic nightclub. The mysterious meeting with Seth had changed her perspective on Campbell Devine and his powers of foresight.

"I recently experienced a sort of vision myself."

"What?" Jack's voice echoed incredulously.

"Don't laugh at me, Jack!" Julee pulled a fist back, ready to smack him on the face.

Campbell, however, didn't react except to shine the spotlight on Julee and ask for her to explain herself. Suddenly thrust into the centre of attention (much to Coryn's continued displeasure), Julee tried to talk without sounding like an idiot:

"Someone spiked my drink when I was out with Reet at The Tronic…"

"WHAT?" Jack shouted, his arms tensing dangerously.

"When did you sneak out to The Tronic?" Coryn's voice was accusing.

Julee raised her fists again in a menacing manner to silence both Jack and Coryn.

"Anyway, as I was saying before I got interrupted," she continued, "someone spiked my drink and I suddenly became aware of Seth's presence close to me. He was as real as any of you here in this room. I got the sense that he wanted to talk to me, he told me things about his death. Things I didn't believe, things I can't forget."

Julee's ghost story, retold in the darkened room, enthralled and fascinated in equal measure. She got to the part of her story which she felt was most relevant.

"Seth told me he cast his spell but it backfired. He said he was, well, 'ensnared between different dimensions' were his exact words. He also told me that Campbell and his powers were absolutely genuine."

Campbell nodded appreciatively. "He said as much to me when I read his future."

"That's not all he told me," Julee said quietly. "He said someone in The Cottage had already attempted to complete the ritual and summon The Infinite."

"It isn't me!" Coryn shrieked.

Something was evidently troubling Lawrence and he spoke his fears aloud.

"If Seth managed to complete the spell, but got shot at some point, then what about those three Ambassadors he went on about?"

"What about them?" Jack said.

"Seth told us on Halloween that when The Infinite is successfully contacted, it sends three ambassadors down to meet the lucky recipient. Campbell had a vision of three dark shapes standing behind Seth. So what happens when they get here and find the person they've travelled all that way to meet is dead?"

"Ah," Campbell Devine squeaked, "that *is* a good question."

Then the lights went back on and everybody gasped a sigh of relief.

Lily came back downstairs when the lights went on again. This was unexpected, because she hadn't managed to inspect the fuse box, but she didn't say anything when she re-entered the living room. The fireplace was roaring again, thanks to Lawrence, and Campbell Devine was still standing in the centre of the room.

She was about to go over and order Campbell to leave when he suddenly swooned and tipped over onto a crumpled heap on the floor. He wasn't unconscious though, he was in severe pain, his hands clutching vainly at his skull.

"Help him!" Julee cried out. "Somebody help him!"

But it wasn't necessary, for Campbell swiftly recuperated from the mysterious pain. He climbed up onto his feet and surveyed everybody with raw bloodshot eyes.

"It was The Ambassadors," he said hoarsely, "they've just sent me a message…"

"A message?" Reet gulped.

"It was one word." Campbell steadied himself on the nearby couch.

"What word?" Julee asked, not sure if she wanted to know.

"Soon."

THE TELEVISION STARES BACK
After The Funeral

Soldier Sam was hiding beneath his bed when the rain of toad started battering his windows. He tried to stifle a scream with his fist, but he ended up biting into his knuckles too hard. It was difficult for him to tell how badly his hands were bleeding, because they were covered in dried up red paint from his graffiti earlier that morning.

The people from The Cottage hadn't listened to him. They hadn't believed what he had said about Seth. They had stood and looked at him as if he was mad, and he knew he wasn't mad. He might be crazy, but not mad. Why wouldn't anyone listen to him?

As Sam hid under the bed, thoughts of the past few days washed over him, becoming a dreamy but painful quilt around his mind. He had seen Seth walking around The Village, which Sam knew was impossible, because Seth was in Bournemouth. Yet Sam knew he had seen him standing outside in the garden. When Sam had looked out of his window, Seth had waved up at him and laughed unkindly.

Sam truly thought the sound of Seth's laughter was the most horrible thing he'd ever heard in his life, it sounded like someone gargling battery acid in their throat. Sam's wife had laughed at him too, but that was before she had left for Bournemouth.

Sam tried ignoring Seth and for a while his tactic worked. His life settled down; he was able to move about without any fuss, things were normal for Soldier Sam. He took his medication from the doctor, he collected his benefits money, and he even bought a new pair of trousers from the charity shop in The Village.

Then one night Seth appeared on Sam's TV and threatened to kill him.

Sam was sitting watching the football when the picture suddenly dissolved. His attempts to fix his battered old television set were doomed to failure. He spent nearly ten minutes trying to work out why his TV had suddenly stopped broadcasting.

Then the static swirled and combined into a familiar form.

"Hello Sam," Seth Kevorkian said cheerfully, "have you seen your wife recently?"

Soldier Sam frantically changed the channel, but he found Seth's face was on every single network. It was impossible to get rid of that face. His horrible laughter echoed from the speakers no matter how often Sam pressed MUTE on the remote control. He finally pulled the plug out of the television…but to Sam's horror *it had no effect whatsoever.*

"I'm coming to get you Sam," Seth hissed from behind the glass.

"No!" Soldier Sam wailed. "NO!"

"You'll like it here in Bournemouth." Seth's voice suddenly turned almost seductive. "You can be with your wife forever and ever. I'm bringing you here soon. Your wife misses you so much. She's so lonely here in Bournemouth. She wants you now."

"NO!"

"The pact was broken!" Seth screamed out of the television.

"The sacrifice was the key to gaining ultimate power and it went wrong because of you!"

"Pl...ple...please!" Sam stuttered for mercy.

"Send them all to Bournemouth," Seth howled, "or run for your life!"

Soldier Sam didn't exactly run, but with the exception of crashing Seth's funeral earlier, he had spent most of the day crouched beneath his bed in terror. It wasn't Seth's voice that echoed in his memories though; it was the voice of his wife Martha. Before the fights and the resentment, Sam loved Martha very much.

("You never admit when you're wrong! I hate you. I don't love you anymore!")

Back in those days Sam was a very different person. Sam occasionally remembered the way he used to be, the way he was before he sent his wife to the place from which no-one ever returns. But his memories played before him like a movie, a film starring an actor who looked like him, but wasn't.

He wanted to be that man again. He *needed* to be that man again.

Soldier Sam slowly crawled out from underneath his bed, his jumbled thoughts finally united into a firm understanding. He chose to ignore Seth's orders. Instead of heading towards The Cottage, he walked in the direction of the police station.

Soldier Sam had a confession to make. Only then could he silence the loud spirit.

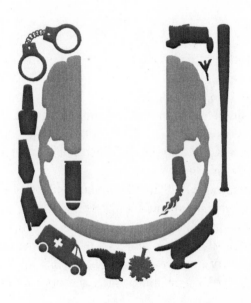

LETTERS FROM THE DEAD
After The Funeral

Coryn was more terrified than she'd ever been in her entire life. She was trapped in The Cottage with a mad psychic from down the street, housemates she didn't like, and it was raining toad outside.

She turned to Campbell and said light-heartedly,

"So what's my future then?"

"Nothing."

"Nothing?!" Coryn shrieked.

"Ever."

Coryn fell onto the nearest couch and buried her face into her hands.

"However, if the world isn't sucked inside out by The Infinite, here's how things will go for you. I'm afraid you don't marry Jack," Campbell said under his breath, so that only Coryn could hear his voice. She appreciated him for sparing her the embarrassment of saying it in front of Jack; she'd already experienced that particular humiliation due to Seth's diary-thieving handiwork.

"Who does Jack marry?"

But Coryn already knew the answer. She wasn't even psychic and yet she knew the obvious answer. It didn't come as a surprise when Campbell motioned gently in the direction of Julee.

"They get married on her twenty-third birthday."

"What happens to me then?" Coryn persisted.

"You get pregnant when you're nineteen and then you'll get your own flat."

"Cool!" Coryn said happily, not seeing the look of dejection on Campbell's face.

Julee was pacing around the living room, waiting for something to happen, wondering how long it would take before Campbell's prediction came to pass.

She suddenly realised that Jack wasn't there with the others.

"Where's Jack? He's not gone out for air again, has he?"

"No," Lawrence said, "he's off upstairs for a few minutes."

Jack was studying the bits of paper he'd taken from Seth's hiding place, completely unaware that someone had sneaked into his room earlier for the same purpose. Most of the sheets of paper were spells and incantations but one of them caught Jack's eye.

It was neatly typed and said:

"I helped you hide the truth about your wife. If you don't pay me £100 for my help, then I'll tell everybody the truth."

Jack continued leafing through other sheets of paper, all with blackmail messages printed on them, his heart pounding furiously and his stomach churning rapidly.

"SAM," one of the other notes started, "Your Wife Isn't in Bournemouth! You better come across with my cash or else!"

"Sam?" Jack mused to himself. "This was being sent to Soldier Sam."

Suddenly the meeting with Sam in the garden and Seth's comment about Sam owing him money made sense. Seth had been blackmailing Soldier Sam. But what was the big secret?

What was big enough to get Sam to hand over his money? What help had Seth given Sam and why did he expect to be paid for it?

Jack was to get an answer to this question when he found another note amongst the pile of paper. He nearly dropped it when a theory unfolded gracefully inside his head, because it suddenly gave him an idea of the kind of danger Seth was putting himself in by sending these blackmail notes.

"Your Wife Isn't In Bournemouth. She's In Your Back Garden. You Killed Her. Give Me £200 And I Won't Tell On You."

The next note was altogether more unusual.

"Does Mother Know You Perform Magick?"

Jack frowned, because that last message obviously wasn't intended for Soldier Sam. He was beginning to form some nasty suspicions about the actual target of the note.

Jack would have read more but the lights went out again.

Then the sound of screaming came from downstairs.

LIGHTS OUT
After The Funeral

In times of dire emergency, the housemates of The Cottage always turned to one person to sort out each and every problem. When Soldier Sam had put in a terrifying appearance at Seth's funeral earlier that day, they had turned to Lily for help. When Campbell Devine had shown up at the front door, they had turned to Lily for help. So who did they call to when the lights went off for the second time that night?

"Lily!" Coryn yelled, her voice echoing eerily in the living room. "Lily!"

"Would you stop screaming in my ears?" Julee snapped irritably. In truth she was terrified and on the verge of asking Lily to do something. The unknown was scary to Julee and right now she was falling into it. She silently cursed Seth for tampering with forces beyond his comprehension, because now he was gone, there wasn't anybody left to blame. Plus she didn't want to ask Lily for help, because Lily was an overbearing pest and she didn't want to be indebted to her.

"The lights have gone out again!" Jack's voice floated into existence.

"That's obvious," Julee retorted.

Even the burning fire, which had warmed everybody by

remaining alight in the living room, had gone out. A hand wrapped itself around Julee's hand; she knew it belonged to Jack because his hands were enormous, just like his arms.

"Let there be light!" a little voice said with a slight chuckle.

Campbell's trusty torch illuminated the large living room. He looked around but found one of them was gone. With narrow eyes the others couldn't see, he directed the beam into the hallway where he could see Lily pacing around nervously.

"Lily!" Coryn cried out. "Are you fixing the lights? Can you hear me?"

Even in the gloom Lily was quite visibly infuriated with Coryn's constant yelling.

"I hear you...Coryn."

The reaction from Coryn was as instantaneous as it was startling. It wasn't the way Lily spoke that sparked such a reaction from Coryn; it was the words she used combined with the murkiness introduced into The Cottage by the blackout. It was all eerily familiar to her and she soon realised where she'd heard a similar voice saying those exact words. Memories of the terrifying events of Halloween flooded back with horrifying clarity; the voice in the forest and how it had taunted her.

"It was *you*," Coryn said in a shuddering voice. "I know it was you."

"What was me?" Lily said in a cold voice.

"It was you on Halloween! I got separated from the others and there was a voice, it spoke to me. It's taken a while for me to place it, but it was you!"

("WHERE ARE YOU?" Coryn screamed at the forest.

WHERE ARE YOU? The forest answered back.

"CAN YOU HEAR ME?" Coryn yelled at the top of her lungs.

I HEAR YOU...CORYN. Something in the forest sighed.)

"It was Lily!" Coryn babbled to the others. "I swear to God

I'm not making it up. She was spying on us in the forest when we cast that spell. She wasn't invited! She left me to be battered by Seth."

If Lily was fazed by Coryn's hysterical accusation, she didn't display it; in fact she was astonishingly calm and collected. Instead of denying the allegation outright, Lily began verbally tearing Coryn to pieces with a ruthless logic and determination.

In a matter of minutes she had Coryn doubting her story.

"You make things up, Coryn. Remember your diary? It's clear you suffer from delusional episodes and the power cut made you recall a previous traumatic event."

Talk of the terrifying events of Halloween also jogged a buried memory for Jack. Something Seth had said that night, and one of the blackmail notes he'd found inside the air vent, suddenly connected into a coherent concept.

"I asked Seth where he got the idea to summon The Infinite."

"I remember that." Julee didn't let go of Jack's hand.

"I remember it too," Lawrence added, "but what did Seth say to you?"

Jack cast his mind back to Halloween so he could repeat the conversation.

("A friend gave me the idea.")

"He said a friend gave him the idea," Jack recalled, "but the way he said it was weird…like it was a joke and only he knew the punch line."

The crumpled sheets of paper in his back pocket suddenly felt heavier. Jack had a very nasty feeling he knew the identity of Seth's other blackmail victim and that, along with Seth's cryptic comments on Halloween, and Coryn's accusation, was enough to convince him there was a traitor in their midst.

Jack decided to test his theory. He faced Lily in the darkness and asked her a simple question, something he'd read only a few minutes beforehand:

"Does Mother know you perform magick?"

Even in the shadows Jack could see the colour draining out of Lily's face. He felt the comforting warmth of Julee's hand leaving him. Before he could prevent it, Julee was pushing herself up into Lily's face with aggressive snarling.

"Seth warned me about you! He told me someone else here was trying to Conjure The Infinite. He was right. You're supposed to be one of us!"

Reet suddenly contributed to the attack on Lily.

"I bet you shot Seth. Campbell's prediction was right all along!"

It was indeed Campbell's opinion that Lily shot Seth Kevorkian. As he stood watching events unfold, he felt the atmosphere in the room slope into a sort of murderous lust. He would have to tread very carefully from now on, because he didn't want to be seen to be encouraging any violence. Visions were swirling behind his eyes, showing him pictures of an uncertain future — a future in which Lily would leave The Cottage and the world drowned in dark magick, courtesy of Seth.

"You've seen the blackmail notes." Lily eyed Jack with an arrogant glare.

"Yes, I have. Seth got the idea to contact The Infinite from you, didn't he?"

Coryn interrupted this exchange, because even though she knew Lily had been in the forest with them on Halloween, she couldn't quite grasp that Lily might be involved in Seth's magickal mumbo jumbo.

"Lily isn't interested in that stuff!" Coryn said skeptically. "That's why we didn't ask her out on Halloween. Now you're saying she's into this magick malarkey."

"She can't cast spells if I break her jaw," Reet said with uncharacteristic menace.

Lawrence was surprised. Yet again Reet had displayed a side of herself that he'd never seen before. He quietly wondered whether or not Lloyd was back again. She had denied it earlier, but the way she was behaving suggested something was wrong.

"Lily," Campbell said smoothly, "I think you had better tell us the whole story."

"Why should I? Nobody will believe any of it."

"Perhaps." Campbell nodded. "But The Ambassadors will be here soon. I've seen the future and things might not end well. The time has come for the truth to be revealed. You owe us that, at the very least."

"Seth Kevorkian…" said Lily between gritted teeth "was a destructive, incompetent, nosy pest. He was constantly taking things that didn't belong to him."

Coryn nodded sympathetically. "My diary," she said bitterly.

"Do you remember I once told you that I too had a diary?" Lily said.

"Yes. You told me you put all of your thoughts in it."

Lily smiled an empty, joyless smile.

"I put more than that in it. I put my spells into it. One of them, the most powerful one, is a spell you've all heard about. It's called Conjuring The Infinite…"

Coryn knew exactly where this story was going.

"Seth stole your diary too."

"Yes. He took it out of my safe."

Reet and Julee looked at each other in mutual understanding. Lily's 'safe' was in fact an old cardboard box stuffed inside a cupboard. No-one else knew that.

"He also stole something else," Lily said suddenly.

"What?" Coryn asked.

"He stole my gun."

WHO SHOT SETH KEVORKIAN?

Lily gasped when she unlocked the safe and witnessed Seth's latest handiwork.

The safe, which was supposedly secure from anybody without the combination, had been plundered. Both her gun and private diary were gone. Lily clenched her fist and thumped the carpet beneath her, hitting out at her frustrations. But it wasn't enough to make her feel better, so she punched the floor three times more.

Lily's training took control and she tried to calm herself. She knew that a clear head was necessary to Conjure The Infinite, and Seth's provocative tactics meant nothing if he couldn't perform the ritual. She had watched with interest on Halloween as he had bungled his first attempt. It didn't matter if he had her books and her gun, he still couldn't do what needed to be done. Lily knew the final step to Conjuring The Infinite was a step too far even for Seth. He lacked her understanding of magick.

And yet the only way he could have broken into her safe was through magick, most likely through some kind of simple unlocking incantation. It astounded Lily how Seth could perform some spells effectively and yet others were beyond him. He'd somehow managed to circumvent the magickal defences she'd put in place.

Thoughts and plans were quickly fashioned in the misty recesses of Lily's psyche. She controlled her breathing until it was steady, and then she climbed up onto her feet. The distant rumble of thunder reached her ears.

Lily turned and followed the sound to its source, her brow furrowing as she contemplated the meaning behind the menacing racket. From her office window, she could see clouds swirling in the distance, a tumultuous sky bursting with lights. It was clear to Lily that powerful forces were being summoned into existence.

Seth was preparing to Conjure The Infinite.

The burning cliffs, thought Seth with immense satisfaction, would be the best place to try and perform the ritual. Secrecy was of the utmost importance. What made the burning cliffs so suitable for his purpose was that his spell wouldn't attract too much attention because the peak was so remote. As he moved higher and higher, Seth's feet trampled on the red heather responsible for giving the cliffs their nickname. He stopped, caught his breath and looked up at the sky, cooling his brow in the wind.

The clouds consented to let the sun shine freely, a corona concerto of breathtaking beauty expanded for those privileged enough to experience it.

"It's too hot," Seth complained as he journeyed across the cliffs.

He didn't realise someone was watching him from a distance.

It didn't take Lily long to reach the foot of the burning cliffs. Anger drove her forwards and upwards, anger at the audacity of the theft. No matter how many times she'd warned him, Seth still continued to break into her property. She'd left fake spells around her office, little traps to tempt him, but it had been the correct spell in her diary he had wanted. And now he held her diary in his possession.

Lily's pursuit was also encouraged by the fear that Seth would succeed in his mission. If he contacted The Infinite, all the years of research and hard work she'd put in would go to waste. The idea of spending the rest of her life working as an agony aunt for a bunch of dumb ungrateful teenagers filled Lily with a depth of despair like no other. She was on the verge of looking into the eyes of eternity, hearing secrets that could collapse whole universes. Lily would finally be able to understand the unfathomable. She couldn't let Seth snatch that from her!

She grimly set about climbing the cliffs, thinking of ways to prevent Seth from running off with her destiny. Her hands ached for her missing gun. If only she could teach the thieving little sod a lesson he would never forget.

A muffled rumbling started up again and Lily speeded up the hunt.

Seth had gained enough altitude to begin the ritual. He was amazed by the awesome beauty of the skyline as he surveyed the world around him like a royal.

"Soon,' Seth said exultantly, "I will king of all things. This will be mine!"

The horizon held his interest until the sound of crashing waves broke him out of his reverie. He brought out the little red book he had stuffed down his shirt and flicked through a few pages, not stopping until he found Lily's neatly written notes. He hadn't bothered bringing any candles; the wind was so ferocious that they wouldn't have ignited anyway. His other hand felt the satisfying weight of the gun he'd liberated from Lily's safe. It was already loaded and ready to be used in the ceremony.

Seth moved his hand away from the gun and he raked the sky with his fingers.

"Etinifni eht fo rewop emilbus eht nopu llac I!"

The ritual had started and nothing would be the same again.

Lily stumbled up the cliffs, gradually edging closer towards her nemesis. Her hair was constantly whipped up by the airstream and fell awkwardly into her eyes, but she kept pushing it away as she climbed higher and higher. She didn't want to be conquered by a teenage twit with a pathetic grasp of sorcery. Speed was of the essence.

A figure hidden nearby surveyed Lily with indifference. She was not the one.

Seth was halfway through the invocation when Lily reached the top of the cliffs.

"Litnu, litnu, litnu revo ssorc lliw eciov ym!"

"Stop what you're doing!"

Seth did exactly as Lily commanded. He then slowly turned to face her, his hair a messy mass of tangles and flapping curls stirred by the mighty winds. He flashed a glorious smile as Lily moved towards him. She didn't notice Seth surreptitiously slip her little red diary under his shirt; she was too busy trying to form words that best articulated her fury.

"You aren't capable of bringing forth The Infinite."

"Well Lily, I don't think that's quite true."

"I have spent nearly ten years researching the arcane knowledge and the incantations. You might have stolen my research, but you don't comprehend it."

Seth laughed at Lily, which she found hugely irritating. She could see from his body language that he felt supreme confidence, the kind of self-assurance that came with true understanding. It suddenly became clear to Lily that Seth was more than able to control the forces he was about to let loose.

Lily tried to bring Seth's confidence down with her trademark directness.

"You failed to Conjure The Infinite on Halloween," she spat dismissively. "You unbalanced the furies and turned nature against you and the others."

Seth's face registered slight surprise at Lily's words. She watched with amusement as the meaning behind her words slowly became clear to him.

"Coryn was right. There *was* someone lurking in the forest on Halloween. It was you all along. You were spying on us, weren't you?"

Lily felt no need to deny the truth any longer:

"Yes! Did you really think I had no idea what you were planning? How many times did I catch you breaking into my office? I knew what you were after. I deliberately left those spells for you to find, because I knew you'd attempt them. I watched as the birds turned on you and the others. I made it happen."

Seth shook his head in wonder as Lily confessed the full extent of her deviousness. He didn't admit it to her face, but he was impressed by the lengths she had gone to in order to scare him away from casting the spell.

"So why are you here?" Seth asked.

Lily didn't reply to his question. He already knew the answer anyway.

"I'm right, aren't I? The correct incantation is in your diary. It was there all along. That's why you're here. You think I'm about to succeed."

Seth studied Lily's reaction and got his reply from her face.

"You've come all this way up the cliffs to stop me."

Thunder rolled across the heavens and strange light peeked through the clouds. Seth seemed to slip into a daydream as all his ambitions and dreams collided. His voice, when he spoke again, was vague:

"I can feel the chains of fate binding me to this moment. This is my destiny."

"Do you know what the spell requires?" Lily's harsh voice cut into his reverie. "Do you know the final step to Conjuring The Infinite? Do you have the guts to do it?"

Seth pulled out a familiar gun and aimed it right at Lily's head. It was the gun he'd taken from her safe. It was apt that Lily had presented herself to him so expediently, thus providing him with an ideal means to complete the final spell.

Lily's eyes looked down the barrel of the gun held in Seth's steady grip.

"I believe your diary mentioned something about a sacrifice," Seth said delightfully. "It's been an addictive read, a thought-provoking experience."

"Fool!" Lily cried out. She was scared now that she had no control over the situation. She had no doubt he would shoot her dead and offer her up to The Infinite. There was no fear in his body language whatsoever. His eyes were wide with awareness. It was a life and death situation; and it would be Seth's life and Lily's death if she didn't so something soon.

"Once I complete the ritual, I shall dispose of you and

then bring forth the power of my master. I will offer him this dimension and beg to rule it in his name. Then I shall have the power to crush this world and all others with a single thought. But I can't stop there, because the real work must begin! I will change everything…"

The sky rumbled and Seth remembered he was halfway through his magick spell.

"Give me the power!" Seth screamed at the universe. "Give me the power!"

Lily watched on with fascination as she witnessed her work being used to devastating effect. She was still scared, but her curiosity was starting to overrule her fear and her mind was beginning to formulate a plan to turn this situation to her advantage.

"Thgir yb enim si taht rewop eht em evig ho!" Seth cried out in the secret language of The Infinite. "Won etinifni eht fo tfig eht em evig!"

Lightning flared down and struck the cliffs with a deafening shriek. The sky melted into a blaze of cold colour, fire and stars. The whirlwind took Seth off his feet and made him fly a few inches off the uneven ground. He screamed happily at his newfound ability to defy gravity. It wasn't much, but it would do for a start.

Then the moment came for the final step, for the completion of the incantation. Seth cocked the trigger of the pistol, ready to end Lily once and for all. This was quite literally a necessary sacrifice, but Seth knew he was going to enjoy ridding himself of the self-important irritant who had pitted her wits against him.

"Goodbye forever," Seth said viciously.

His index finger delicately squeezed the trigger of the gun…

Lily threw up her hands and shouted:

"MUNDARA!"

Seth pulled the trigger of the gun only to find he no longer held that gun. His expression was almost comical as he did a double-take, looking around him to see if he'd dropped it. But it didn't take Seth long to discover the gun's whereabouts.

Lily had it pointed directly at him, a strangely satisfied smile on her face.

"You've mastered the Transmat spell," Seth said uneasily.

Lily laughed a glorious laugh. "Obviously."

The lurking figure was equally baffled by the miracle he'd just witnessed. It had to be a trick of some kind! He pondered whether or not the girl with the gun would send the nasty boy all the way to Bournemouth. *Perhaps*, the watcher thought worriedly, *perhaps he'll meet my wife there?*

"You've tested my theories in person, so I thank you for that, but I'm afraid I can't let you return to The Cottage. I've tired of your constant attempts at blackmail and larceny. You've caused me far too much trouble to let you go now."

Seth looked horrified at the dramatic shift in his fortunes. He was incredibly close to gaining ultimate power and now Lily was ready to step in and take what rightfully belonged to him. It wasn't fair! His mind raced frantically but thoughts weren't coming to him, it was desperately empty of tricks and retorts.

"Please…" Seth begged Lily.

"Where is my diary?" Lily demanded sharply.

"I've left it in my room back at The Cottage!" Seth told her. "It's in my hiding place along with all the blackmail notes. I'll take you to it if you like."

"No, I think I'll retrieve it on my own."

Lily fired a bullet directly into Seth's chest. He screamed once and went down. The sky roared with approval and she dropped the gun to the ground.

Lily waited for a sign that she had completed the invocation but she was disappointed to experience nothing but the start of a heavy downpour and a windstorm.

"The eyes of the sky will open!" Lily cried out into the heavens.

But there was nothing at all but the grinding disappointment of failure. Lily ran over to Seth's corpse and kicked it ferociously. She knelt and placed her index finger on Seth's neck, feeling for a pulse, but her fingers felt naught.

Lily stood up and threw the gun, then she fled the scene of the crime, hoping against all odds that any evidence would be destroyed by the storm. But she had not thrown the gun far enough.

Seth Kevorkian opened his eyes and laughed wickedly.

MADNESS, MAGICK AND MURDER
After The Funeral

The silence in The Cottage was as desolate as the darkness which enveloped it. Lily's confession had shaken everybody profoundly, the mystery of their fallen housemate had finally been solved, but nobody took any pleasure in the news of Seth's demise.

"Seth stole a gun from your safe," Jack said with comprehension. "That explains the bullets I found in Seth's room."

"Did you find my diary?" Lily asked quickly.

"It wasn't there," Jack replied, "just the bullets and the notes."

"I trusted you," Lawrence said indignantly. "I really did."

"It wasn't personal," Lily said, relieved to have finally confessed her role in Seth's murder. "I might have trained as a psychologist but my interest in magick has been constant, indeed the cultural connection between magick and psychology stretches back into the dark ages…"

"I wish you'd stop going on about being a psychologist. We all know the truth. Mother isn't here to protect you, Lily. Don't forget that."

Nobody said anything to contradict Julee's sudden outburst.

Everyone in the room waited for Lily's reaction, but she deliberately chose to ignore Julee.

"He broke into my office…"

Julee interrupted Lily once again and stated in no uncertain terms that she wasn't going to play along with the charade any more.

"Shut your mouth! It's all lies that come out of it. How can you criticize anyone for lying? All you ever do is lie and I can't stand it anymore!"

Lily screamed and covered her ears, not willing to submit to the truth.

"He broke into my office and rifled through my things so he could get ideas to blackmail me!" She shrieked pathetically. "He was going to get dirt on everybody in The Cottage. Your files are in my office. Seth would have gone through them and used the information to intimidate every single person in this room. You lot should be grateful for my intervention!"

Campbell felt this was a rather odd manner for a social worker, but he said nothing. The housemates obviously had a lot of issues to work through.

"Why did you have a gun anyway?" Julee enquired.

"I didn't want to get my clothes and nails messy during the ceremony. A sacrifice is required in order to summon The Infinite into this realm. A bullet wound is neater than a knife wound, isn't it?"

There was a stark, horrified silence from everyone in the room. Surprisingly, it was Coryn who spoke on behalf of the majority.

"You shot Seth for the sake of your *magick* ceremony?"

Lily shook her head with furious disbelief at what she felt was Coryn's insincerity.

"You all wanted him dead at some point!"

"You don't have the right to lecture us!" Jack yelled, his arms tensing perilously. "You nearly killed all of us on Halloween, you stupid bitch!"

"She's not a bitch," Campbell corrected Jack's impolite comment, "she's a witch."

"She's not a witch," Coryn snapped.

There was a period of quiet as everyone waited for someone to say something else.

"I haven't had a cigarette all night," Julee said abruptly.

"I didn't know you smoked!" Lily said in genuine surprise.

"I didn't know you had a gun stashed away in your bedroom," Julee countered.

Campbell felt somewhat bewildered by the sudden turn of events against Lily, but his surprise was soon replaced by something more urgent.

The room had acquired a new vibe, a prevailing malevolence that was playing havoc with his psychic wavelengths. He found himself engulfed with nausea as his head flared in pain, as if something had reached into his skull and squeezed; it was nearly as bad as the pain he'd suffered earlier on that same night when The Ambassadors sent their celestial telegram.

The residents didn't notice his discomfort. They were all too busy bickering in the corner. Jack yelled something at Lily, who retaliated with a snide comment about his dad, and then Reet got involved, which provoked Lawrence into defending her.

Campbell Devine didn't join in the dispute. He was preoccupied by the sight of three shapes materializing in the centre of the room. He tried to alert the others, but his voice was drowned out by their loudness. They only stopped when Julee realised something was wrong with the little psychic from down the road.

There wasn't a sudden explosion of hellfire and smoke. The Ambassadors of The Infinite simply appeared out of nowhere, heralded by the beating of wings. They were angels, beautiful and bright. Their unfurled wings spanned the entire space of the living room. The contrast between their ghostly forms and the snug living room was glaring. They made for an imposing sight. They were all things to all men. They were demigods, already ancient when the universe itself had been newborn. They were also unseen and unheard by everyone in The Cottage.

Everyone, that is, with the exception of Campbell Devine.

"They're standing right there!" Campbell insisted.

"I can't see anything," Lily said hesitantly.

"They're standing right there I tell you!"

Campbell looked around the room for Julee, who had become something of an ally over the course of the evening. How could she not see what he was seeing? But when his eyes reached her face, he found her reaction disheartening; she didn't look particularly impressed. Campbell didn't understand what was happening. He looked back towards the source of the glow and the three figures blinked back at him.

"You honestly can't see them?" Campbell asked, his voice breaking slightly.

"There's nothing there," Julee replied. There was a quality in her voice, something Campbell disliked passionately. He soon identified it as sympathy. It was clear Julee didn't believe him. Not only that but she felt sorry for him.

She was undoubtedly regretting her previous support for him.

Jack put forward his own little theory on what was happening.

"Maybe they're here but they're invisible."

"YES!" Campbell declared excitedly. It was the one explanation that could save his credibility.

But Lily quickly dismissed Jack's theory in her usual blunt manner.

"If The Ambassadors were to arrive here, they would reveal themselves to me. They wouldn't appear before a pretend psychic with crap taste in fashion. I am, after all, one of the initiated. I gave Seth the idea to contact The Infinite."

Reet stepped away from the fireplace she'd been standing at and motioned towards Campbell. She wanted to say something important. But something very strange happened in the millisecond it took for her to speak. Suddenly it wasn't Reet by the fireplace, it was Seth Kevorkian! This miasma lasted until Campbell blinked it away. Then Reet was standing before him for a second time, smiling sweetly. It must have been a trick of the light, Campbell reasoned. He was seeing Seth everywhere.

"Are The Ambassadors really in this room with us?" Reet enquired.

"They are, my dear."

"But we just can't see them?"

"I can see them," Campbell said, but he wasn't so confident now.

"Just because they're invisible, it doesn't mean they aren't here. If they are actually here, I should be able to go over and touch them. Isn't that right?"

Campbell couldn't fault Reet's logic, so he waited as she walked towards the Ambassadors. She seemed confident, her trust in his abilities absolute. The others stood in the background, spellbound as their pixie-haired housemate moved cautiously towards the centre of the room, nearer to the spot where Campbell swore The Ambassadors held court.

There was a loud gasp of disappointment from the others as

Reet passed through The Ambassadors.

As far as the residents of The Cottage were concerned, Reet had just walked around an empty living room. But from Campbell's perspective, it was far different; Reet had passed through the three creatures. Their ghostly outlines had shifted and blurred, rippling away until she had rejoined her housemates.

"There's nothing here," Reet announced. She looked disillusioned.

"You just walked through them!"

The Ambassadors of The Infinite giggled, but only Campbell could hear them.

Julee put a hand on Campbell's shoulder, a friendly gesture that he found irritating.

"Don't patronize me!" Campbell shook her away. "I know what I see!"

"That doesn't mean anything," Lily said haughtily. "It might be real to you, but that doesn't mean it actually *is* real. You're breathing the same air as a bunch of pill-popping manic depressives, alcoholics, and schizophrenics. You've been drinking tea with a bunch of crazy teenage washouts. It seems *I'm* the only sane one here."

Lawrence burst out laughing. Campbell felt he was missing something important.

"Please don't attempt to psychoanalyze me. I assure you I'm quite sane."

"You claimed to see the end of the world in a vision!"

One of the angels spoke but its voice was a hissing, spitting, vicious thing of horror.

"Where is the warlock?"

"Did you hear that?" Campbell yelped excitedly.

The angel spoke again, directing many voices towards Campbell.

"We are here to complete the deal."

"They want Seth!"

"Where is the warlock?" one of the angels repeated.

"Where is he?" the other angel said.

"Bring us the errant warlock or you will all die horribly."

"I can't see or hear anything," Julee said, aghast at Campbell's conduct.

Lily laughed, unwilling to hide her satisfaction with the latest turn of events.

"He's as mad as us if he's hearing voices in his head," she said to the others.

"The voice in my head resents that implication," Reet snapped irritably.

Julee backed away from Campbell, another sign that she wasn't sure whether or not to trust him anymore. He was trying desperately to regain the admiration and trust his visions had afforded him and the position in the house they had afforded him. Lily hadn't made any secret of her distrust. But Campbell had accurately predicted several events throughout the course of the evening. It was time to remind the others of his abilities.

"I told you all that someone in The Cottage shot Seth."

"You were right," Julee admitted, "Lily has admitted shooting him."

Jack tried to apply rationality to the situation. This, of course, wasn't his forte. But on this occasion he actually made a very good point.

"As Seth was murdered by someone with a gun," he said, "the chances of his killer being someone he knew and lived with weren't too far-fetched." He looked at Campbell apologetically. "You could have made a lucky guess."

The Ambassadors laughed again, causing Campbell to scowl at them. They were relishing his embarrassment.

"What about the freak weather I predicted earlier?"

Nobody could explain away that particular prediction. The weather had calmed throughout the night, but the streets outside were still full of displaced toad.

An idea suddenly occurred to Campbell. It was far-fetched but it helped explain the peculiar state of affairs he was currently fighting against.

"The Ambassadors are here in this room, but they've journeyed to this realm as...psychic projections of some sort. Only a highly sensitive psychic can see them!"

Lily, however, was having none of it.

"That's all very convenient considering you're the only psychic in the village."

Campbell was about to shout a very nasty insult at the supercilious social worker when two bright spotlights hit her in the chest. They moved across the room, bending and melding into cracks and crevices until they abruptly vanished.

Coryn screamed fearfully, startled by the brightness of the twin beams.

"Is it The Ambassadors?" she cried out in terror.

Campbell looked over at the trio of angels, but they remained impassive.

"I don't think so. It looks like the headlights of a car."

There was a new sound in the darkness. Everybody in The Cottage stood rooted to the floor, waiting for the source to reveal itself. Footsteps moved up the gravel outside, towards the main door of the building. The living room was situated next to the hall, which meant someone was round the corner.

"Who could it be?" Campbell whispered urgently.

"You're the psychic," Lily hissed back at him, "you should know."

The room was gloomy, save the sickly green glow cast by The Ambassadors, a light visible only to Campbell's eyes. He looked around to see Jack tensing himself for a fight, his default reaction whenever he felt endangered.

Someone stepped into the living room. They reached up to the light switch...

The Ambassadors vanished as the room was engulfed by brightness.

It was Mother. Her face was pale and she looked slightly dazed.

"I know what really happened to Seth. I know who killed him."

Understandably, the others felt Mother had missed the boat on this one.

CONJURING THE INFINITE

Seth felt as if the ferocity of the winds might strip the skin off his bones. He climbed unsteadily onto his feet and breathed a huge sigh of relief when he realised he was still in one piece. But how had he survived? His hands quickly felt all around his body, searching for evidence that he had been shot, until he found the little red diary in his breast pocket.

It had a small indentation on it, the mark of a deflected bullet.

Seth doubled over in hysterical laughter. He kissed the lucky little spell book and held it above his head with a dramatic flourish. If surviving a bullet wasn't a good omen, what was? It made Seth more determined than ever to complete the ritual.

But the wind had other plans for the stolen diary: a massive gust plucked the book from Seth's fingers and sent it hurtling over the cliff edge.

"No!" Seth cried out. "No! No! No!"

Then a random thought stopped him in his tracks, something he hadn't seen but heard. Lily had shot him dead, intending him as a sacrifice for The Infinite; but obviously he wasn't dead, thus the spell couldn't process itself properly.

"She dropped the gun!" Seth exclaimed happily. "She dropped it!"

He stooped, desperately looking around the cliffs for the discarded gun, but a pair of booted feet walked into view. It wasn't Lily though. She was long gone.

It was Soldier Sam. And the gun was secure in his hands.

"What are you doing here?" Seth yelled above the mournful wind.

"Have you seen my wife?" Soldier Sam asked pleasantly.

"HELLO!" Seth shouted to get his voice heard. "Nobody has seen your wife because she's dead and buried. You put her in the ground. I told you to tell people she'd gone to Bournemouth. It was my idea! Remember?"

Soldier Sam burst into tears and waved the gun dangerously.

"She's gone to Bournemouth!" he yelled.

"Idiot!" Seth hastily backed away from the gun. "You killed her."

"No! She's gone far away to Bournemouth with all the others..."

Seth raised an eyebrow at Soldier Sam's irrational comment. Things were beginning to spiral out of control, the situation becoming unmanageable. Seth knew just how unstable Sam Carrickstone was, he had actively encouraged Sam's madness across recent months for his own ends, but now Sam had a loaded gun at his disposal.

Seth knew he had to be extremely cautious.

"Give me the gun," Seth said in a sugary voice, "Please Sam. Give me the gun and I promise I'll send you on a one-way trip to Bournemouth."

"No!" Sam wiped tears away with his dirty coat sleeve. "I won't do it."

Seth's polite tones suddenly took on a harsh quality as his anger surfaced.

"You are a stupid, smelly, irrelevant booze bag! Give me the damn gun or else!"

Sam wailed as the hateful words cut into the darkest recesses of his memory.

("I don't love you anymore! I want a divorce! Stay away from me Sam!")

"She's gone to Bournemouth! She's dead! She's gone to B...B...Bournemouth!"

"Are you an a...a...alcoholic or what?" Seth mocked cruelly as Sam fought with his inner demons.

Sam slammed the gun against his head, hitting it off his skull again and again. If Seth hadn't had a gun pointed at him, he might have enjoyed Sam's distress a little bit longer, but time was running out and Seth needed to finish the spell now.

Seth lunged at the gun. It was his first and final mistake.

Sam effortlessly countered Seth's attack by bringing the gun down with enough force to smash Seth onto the ground. The barrel flashed and made contact with the left side of Seth's face, and this and the heavy wind brought him down with ease.

"You'll pay for this!" Seth moaned as pain overwhelmed him.

("I'm leaving you for your brother! He knows how to treat a woman!")

"You've been sending me notes," Soldier Sam said quietly, "signing them with my wife's signature. But I know it can't be her. She's dead."

When Seth spoke again, it was in a language Soldier Sam didn't comprehend:

"Etinifni eht fo rewop emilbus eht nopu llac I!"

There was an explosion somewhere in a faraway dimension. The universe stopped and waited to discover what would happen next.

"Litnu, litnu, litnu revo ssorc lliw eciov ym!"

Seth rose slowly to his feet, confidence returning. His arms rose towards the sky.

"Srefsnart rewop eht dna yawa skool esrevinu eht!"

Soldier Sam didn't have a handle on what was taking place before his eyes, but somewhere deep inside a gut feeling cried out to him. Everything in the core of his being could feel the concentrated vibration of evil in its purest form. It surrounded Soldier Sam. It was the sky, the cliffs, the trees, the wind, the rain...but most of all it was Seth.

"Thgir yb enim si taht rewop eht em evig ho!"

The sky shattered and Reason fled the cosmos alongside its brother, Chaos. The laws of everything civilised and good and pure were subverted. The heavens tilted upside down. The furies unbalanced and the greatest powers in creation warped into something innovative. Then the power of The Infinite rinsed through the whole of the world; its philosophies proving valid, if only for now. It waited for a reply.

"Won etinifni eht fo tfig eht em evig!" Seth's voice echoed across time and space.

The darkening sky cast a dramatic shadow across the cliffs. Soldier Sam looked up to see the sun blotted out of the sky by a gargantuan presence. He had never seen anything like it, not even in his worst nightmares:

Two golden eyes peered down from outside the universe, becoming the horizon and the entire world around them.

"The eyes of the sky have opened!" Seth hollered victoriously.

Although Sam wasn't aware of it, 'the eyes of the sky' were in fact the eyes of The Infinite, looking down at the one who had summoned it. The eyes didn't see Sam though, they were only for Seth, and nothing else in the cosmos mattered.

Light seemed to cascade from the eyes, from the stars above the cliffs, and the mystic downpour was absorbed by Seth Kevorkian, his face twisted in pleasure and pain as apparitions of power were presented to him. He was intoxicated by the strength of the aurora borealis, that much was clear to Soldier Sam, and when Seth spoke again his voice had adopted a higher timbre.

He was being slowly transformed into something far superior. His blue eyes blinked, but they were no longer blue, they were gold just like those of The Infinite.

"I can hear clouds drifting across the sky! The worms beneath my feet…demand freedom from the darkness…the secret hopes of humankind…all of it trivial. I can see into other worlds…other universes…they're calling out to me. They've always called to me! I never knew that until now, but now I know everything. I KNOW EVERYTHING!"

Seth wasn't exaggerating — he was cosmically connected to a higher authority, the connection inflating his awareness, swelling it into a preview of what was to come.

But this all came at a terrible price. Seth had one last task to undertake to complete his mission.

"A sacrifice must be made!" a voice called to Sam from across a tornado. "I have to complete the ritual. The Infinite demands it in order for me to seal the deal."

Soldier Sam replied with just one word. It told Seth everything he needed to know.

"Bournemouth."

The stolen gun was raised and three shots were fired.

The eyes of the sky closed over and the world dissolved back to its original state. Soldier Sam stood alone on the cliffs, a gun in his hand and a body at his feet.

A rare moment of clarity came to Sam's jumbled thoughts. He looked down at the bloodied corpse on the ground and the gun suddenly felt too heavy for his grip. He swung around in a clean arc and tossed the gun into the sky, watching with grim satisfaction as the wind took it into the sea forever.

Then Sam ran back home and pretended to forget about Seth Kevorkian.

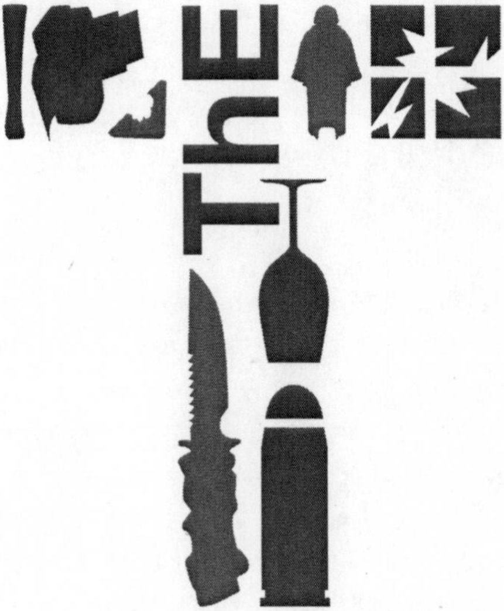
ThE

A GOOD STRONG DOSE
OF REALITY
After The Funeral

Nobody uttered a word as Mother explained how the police had come to the hospital to tell her about Soldier Sam's confession. He had gone to the station earlier that night and confessed his role in Seth's murder. Not only that but he'd given them detailed descriptions of how it had all happened.

There could be no doubt that Sam was telling the truth.

Lily quickly reasserted her position within the group dynamic, approaching Mother as an equal. None of the others knew what to say; after all, they'd just heard Lily confessing to Seth's murder. Yet Mother was assuring them Soldier Sam was the culprit. Who was telling the truth? The only definite was no-one knew for sure.

"How did you get back here?" Lily asked amiably.

"Celia from the community centre gave me a lift up in her car," Mother said.

"Celia Grossman?" Jack asked, his voice betraying confusion. Another contradiction; Seth had told him all about Celia, and how he set the community centre on fire just to spite her. He couldn't understand why Celia would drive Mother all the way back up to The Cottage if she hated the place so much.

"Yes, Celia was kind enough to drive me through that terrible weather."

Lily ambushed the conversation.

"But why are you back?"

Mother looked straight across the living room at Lily. Jack, however, looked away.

"I didn't get a chance to organize cover when I was taken to the hospital. But I couldn't leave you all on your own. Goodness knows what might happen without my being here, besides…the injuries I suffered weren't as bad as they first appeared."

Mother suddenly seemed to realise there was a stranger in her midst. She recoiled at the sight of Campbell's tacky gold suit. It was the vilest thing she'd seen in her life.

"Who are you?" she inquired. "What are you doing here at The Cottage?"

Campbell didn't appreciate her tone of voice. He gripped onto the lapels of his suit jacket and craned his head upwards, giving his own impression of contemptuousness. He'd dealt with officious people such as this before in his life. The only way to come out on top against bureaucrats was to become equally uncompromising.

But Campbell didn't get the chance to answer Mother's questions. Lily intervened yet again, her voice condemning.

"He's the psychic from the village. He's kindly came all the way here to help avert the apocalypse. Seth, it turns out, cast a magick spell and three monsters from another dimension are here as a result."

Even as she spoke, Campbell had to admit to himself how fanciful it all sounded.

"I can see I was right to return as soon as I did," Mother remarked coldly.

"I know this must seem rather far-fetched, but I assure you my powers are genuine. I came here to warn everyone that Seth did indeed cast a powerful incantation. Not only that, but I've got a strong psychic feeling that we're all in danger from someone standing in this room."

His remark seemed to remind everyone about the danger in their midst.

"Soldier Sam didn't shoot Seth, it was Lily!" Julee piped up.

"Yes," Lily agreed, "I did. He had to die. The power of The Infinite was mine."

Mother was incredulous at the revelation. Her jaw dropped as everyone started fighting again. She was still trying to process the idea of a psychic in her home; it wasn't every night she returned to find a cuckoo in the nest.

"Lily shot Seth because he was attempting to contact The Infinite…"

"I found bullets in Seth's room…"

"You were there in the forest that night…"

"The Ambassadors were standing over there as real as you and I…"

"He sent a mystical distress signal to another dimension…"

"He spoke to me through the pipes…"

"Does anyone know if the shop is open this time of night? I'm gasping for a…"

Mother could take no more of this madness, so she did what any other professional person in her situation would do.

She screamed at everybody to SHUT UP.

The power in Mother's voice instantly ended the undignified battle and she effortlessly took charge of the patients.

"I take it you've been stirring them up, encouraging their delusions?"

Campbell realised she was talking to him.

"As opposed to you," he shot back.

"You are filling their heads with nonsense about magick spells and psychic powers!"

"Never mind that," Campbell shouted back at her, "You should ask your second in command over there (he pointed at Lily) why she kept a gun in her office. She's completely unbalanced and you gave her a job here in The Cottage."

"What gun? I have no idea what you're talking about."

Campbell wanted to scream but he managed to keep his irritation under control. Composure was important when dealing with someone as well-connected as Mother. He was becoming dizzy, going around in circles with the woman.

"Lily shot Seth. Not only did she admit it, but I saw it with my own eyes."

"You actually witnessed Lily shooting Seth with a gun?"

"Yes, in a vision."

Mother shook her head negatively. She couldn't believe what she was hearing. Ideas of various available treatments were springing to mind, because she couldn't believe Campbell Devine was being serious. Not only did he need help, it was obvious he needed *her* help.

"Whether or not you believe in my abilities is irrelevant," Campbell snapped tetchily. "You still left that fruit loop over there (he pointed at Lily again) in charge of your patients. Your judgment deserves to be called into question for that alone."

Mother sighed, a sign of weariness and inevitability. The time had come to clear up a few misconceptions about Lily and the important work of The Cottage. This ridiculous little man needed a dose of reality, and he needed it right away.

"I don't need to tell you this, Mr. Devine, but some of the treatments used in the recuperation of my patients are experimental in nature. Lily has lived here in The Cottage longer than the others. As a result, she's taken on a persona. She believes herself to be a fully qualified social worker. I indulge some of her fantasies, indeed we all do as a matter of course. But I fear I might have gone too far."

Campbell couldn't believe what he was hearing.

"You mean to tell me she *isn't* your second in command?"

"She isn't even a social worker," Mother admitted ruefully, "but the others are under strict instructions not to interfere with her treatment."

"But she killed Seth," Jack said. "The bullets…"

"Sam killed Seth!" Mother yelled. "He has already told the police he did it."

Lily crossed her arms and frowned as they argued over the murder.

"I dropped the gun at the scene of the crime," Lily said. "He must have found it."

"Lily," Mother started. "There's someone in this room I'd like you to psychoanalyze. They desperately need some perspective and I think you can offer it."

"Of course," Lily said in the voice she'd used all night. "Who is it?"

Campbell crossed his arms, waiting for Mother to set Lily loose on him. But it didn't happen, instead Mother did something extraordinary. She surprised him. Instead of getting Lily to psychoanalyze Campbell, she instead put Lily's talents to use on someone else completely:

"I'd like for you to psychoanalyze *yourself*, Lily."

There was a faint gasp from someone in the room. Campbell wasn't sure, but he thought it sounded like Lawrence, although it could have been Reet. They were always together, encircling in each other's centre of gravity.

The effect of Mother's kindly request on Lily was instantaneous.

It was quite a remarkable thing to witness. Lily started giving the session serious consideration, and she rattled off a list of her own mental problems in front of everyone.

"Despite outward appearances," she said, "Lily Myers is motivated by irrational impulses. She's quite possibly delusional. These unconscious conflicts would create lasting neurotic tendencies as well as other mental disturbances. Defence mechanisms would result in compulsive lying and transference."

"Bloody hell," Campbell said incredulously.

"Do you understand why I have problems believing anything Lily supposedly told you all tonight?" Mother said quietly. "Who is going to believe Lily supplied the gun Sam used to shoot Seth? Who will believe anyone from The Cottage? None of you are credible witnesses. You're all as untrustworthy and erratic as each other!"

Mother quickly added, "And some are more erratic than others."

Campbell caught a sideways glance from her as she said it. His face went cherry red.

"What about the weather?" Julee asked. No-one had managed to clarify that strange occurrence to her complete satisfaction. Mother, as usual, had a rational explanation that made complete sense to her.

"It was caused by a typhoon from India."

"Mother, come on!"

Mother lifted her hands up in a placating manner. Campbell watched in admiration as she skillfully controlled the different emotions of the housemates, soothing them with her words whilst overwhelming their antagonism with her personality.

"I know it all sounds unbelievable, but tonight's news reported it. They had experts in the studio. It was caused by a typhoon, and that's a fact."

"Then what happened tonight had nothing to do with Seth?"

Everyone in the room looked at Reet, who had fallen onto a chair. She didn't look healthy at all. It was as if the events of the evening had taken the heaviest toll on her. She looked up, her eyes dark beneath a jagged fringe.

Campbell backed away in disgust as three shapes liquefied into existence behind her.

The Ambassadors of The Infinite had finally returned from the ether. Their eyes radiated light as they encircled Reet, but they did nothing more than stand in position around her. It was an eerie, unsettling sight for Campbell. For some reason he couldn't fathom, a great many of his visions centred on Reet.

"They're back!" he cried out.

Jack, Lawrence, Julee, and Coryn didn't move. They'd all grown bored of Campbell's theatrics and wanted the night to be over with.

"Perhaps you were right to come to The Cottage," Mother said abruptly.

Desperate and afraid, Campbell took his eyes off the three entities surrounding Reet, and he looked over at the stern face of Mother.

"I think you need help," she said in a smooth voice. She sounded gracious, as though he would be doing himself a favour if he chose to remain for treatment.

"You're lost in fantasy, Mr. Devine, just like Lily and the other patients here in The Cottage. I've made my career out of helping people like you. There are opportunities for help here, but only if you allow yourself to get that help."

No-one in the room failed to spot the significance of the word 'if'. Every single one of them had heard it during their initial induction into Cottage life. Mother's so-called pep talk had gradually become something of a private joke between the occupants. Instead of being life-affirming, as she obviously intended, it came across as condescending.

"I don't need your help," Campbell spat.

The Ambassadors suddenly launched into fierce debate, but it was in a language that no human could ever understand. Their frenzied babbling fluttered across the room and reached his ears and only his ears. The others still couldn't see or hear them. Campbell tried to block out the psychic noise, but it was a futile gesture.

"They want Seth," he said between gritted teeth. "They haven't changed their minds about that!"

With that said Mother turned on the spot and stormed out of the room, moving towards the front door. She opened it and motioned for Campbell to leave.

As Campbell slowly left the living room, Julee placed a hand on his arm and stopped him. She had one last thing to say:

"Remember your prediction from earlier? You said someone here would leave The Cottage tonight and never return again…"

Not only did Campbell recall that prediction, but he also knew exactly what Julee had taken it to mean. It was obvious she'd reached her own conclusion.

"It's you, Campbell. You're going to leave us and never return."

"Goodbye, my dear." He said sadly.

Somewhere behind Campbell, from the furthest end of the room, demonic laughter echoed and followed him as he walked through the main door to a bleak winter night.

The laughter stopped when Mother slammed the door behind him.

As Campbell walked down the gravel path away from The Cottage, he stopped just for a moment and looked back at the old building. He caught a glimpse of the future. But this wasn't a psychic premonition. It was a forewarning of where he might end his days if he wasn't careful. He'd seen the end of the world. He'd encountered creatures from another universe, the sort of monsters science couldn't explain. He'd watched events he'd seen in his visions play out before his eyes. And in the end he didn't know whether any of it was real.

But what if it *was* real? That was the unsettling question that he couldn't answer.

Campbell glanced down at his horrible gold suit, and suddenly he despised himself. Everything he represented was a silly, awful joke. How could he have hoped to prevent Armageddon? He was a school dropout with barely a qualification to his name. He'd become a ludicrous person since setting up his business.

And yet strange things had happened tonight, inexplicable things he'd witnessed with his own eyes. Could it all have been tricks of the light, phantasmagoria, illusion?

"It *has* to be real," he said forcefully, a final attempt at convincing himself.

Campbell resumed his journey back to the village. He turned his back on The Cottage and moved away from the crazy people who lived inside. As he crunched the gravel with his feet, he failed to notice something fluttering past him, carried by a gust of wind. It must have floated out of The Cottage before the door slammed shut.

A solitary white feather plucked
from the wing of an angel.

For the first time in a long time,
Campbell didn't know what the future held.

FOREVER FRIEND

Soldier Sam's confession didn't take too long. Some of the attending officers, the ones who knew Soldier Sam from living in the village, were more surprised at the profound change in his personality than they were his declaration of guilt.

For a start, he spoke to them clearly and concisely, in full sentences with a firm voice and directness that just wasn't like him at all.

"I killed my wife Martha," he said, "and buried her in our garden. Then Seth arrived in my life and everything changed. He knew about the murder. He offered to help me keep my secret. He told me to tell the village that Martha had moved to Bournemouth and she wasn't coming back. He was very specific about it."

Sam closed his eyes as painful emotions were keenly felt for the first time in years.

"Then he started demanding money for 'services rendered'. He used to joke that blackmailing me was his part-time job. In the end I followed him up to the cliffs and killed him too. I got a gun...I can't remember where I got it from...but I shot him. I don't think he expected me to do it, but I did and I'm here to take the consequences of my actions."

In the distance, a crack of lightning split the sky, and Soldier Sam felt The Ambassadors departing from this dimension.

Sam peered out of the nearby cell window, his thoughts moving slowly towards The Cottage, and Seth Kevorkian, of course.

Mother locked the doors after casting Campbell Devine out from The Cottage. It had been a long day and an even longer night for everybody. Tired emotionally and physically, everybody headed for bed.

Everybody, that is, except one of the housemates.

Reet slowly closed her bedroom door and headed back into her en suite bathroom. She clicked the bathroom light on and walked over towards the mirror on the wall. Despite feeling frightened in the same bathroom earlier on that night, she no longer felt fear; in fact she no longer felt anything other than wicked amusement. She gazed into the mirror and studied her face with wide eyes.

("There is a voice in your ear.")

Reet had a strange suspicion that Campbell suspected the truth about her, but it didn't matter anyway, no-one believed him. He didn't believe in himself any longer.

The boundless depths of the mirror captivated Reet. She raised her hand and gave her mirror image a little merry wave hello.

Seth Kevorkian waved back.

"Lloyd is gone," he said with a splendid smile. "A new occupant has moved in."

"Hello Seth," Reet said calmly. "How are you today?"

His voice was whiny but Reet didn't mind. He was her reflection now.

"I'm so bored," he sighed, "I want to have some fun."

Then he paused, as though unsure whether or not to broach a certain subject.

"Are The Ambassadors gone?"

"Yes. I pretended not to see them, just like you asked."

"Good," Seth hissed, "I thought they would look inside your head like they did Campbell's. They might have found me hiding here *and I must never be found*. Why should I serve The Infinite? This is the kind of power I want…the power to strike unseen at my enemies. I will have revenge on everybody that crossed me! Lily will be the first. I'm going to send that bitch to Bournemouth in a body bag. And nobody will suspect me, because I'm officially dead."

Reet laughed as Seth's thoughts bled into her thoughts, mixing them together, their desires and ambitions becoming one as Seth attempted to seize complete control.

"I wanted to sacrifice Lily to The Infinite," he explained using Reet's lips and her voice. "My original plan was to use her, but Sam conveniently arrived after she fled the scene. I decided to sacrifice him, but he shot me and I became the sacrifice in his place! He fundamentally altered the dynamics of the spell. But instead of dying, I became something else entirely. Hiding inside your head is very easy. I nearly slipped up tonight at dinner when I ordered chicken, I forgot you only eat rabbit food."

Seth laughed spitefully as Reet attempted to resist his will.

"We'll make a great team, you and I."

Reet tried to scream but the muscles in her face ignored her frantic thoughts as full possession finally took hold. The sound of malicious laughter filled the little bathroom, squeezing out every bit of silence, but it wasn't Reet's modest laughter, it was the girlish cackle of Seth Kevorkian.

"Yes," he said seconds later, "we'll be forever friends."

ABOUT THE AUTHOR

Kirkland Ciccone writes and performs quirky one man shows for any theatre or venue lucky enough to have him. It wasn't always this way though. He left school bored and restless, plotting to become a journalist until the time came for him to make a choice — performing arts or writing stories about jumble sales. Fact, in Kirkland's case, is always weirder than fiction. He has written for cool music 'zines such as This Is Fake DIY, Rock Louder, Neu Magazine, and Subba Cultcha. His previous shows include In Bed with Kirkland Ciccone, The Dead Don't Sue, A Secret History, Kirkland Ciccone Plays Pop and others.

This is his first novel.

Kirkland lives in Falkirk with his dog Lord Fanny.
He is currently writing his next novel.

For news on upcoming novels, events, and general juvenilia:

www.kirklandciccone.co.uk
www.twitter.com/kirklandciccone

BAD FAITH
Gillian Philip

Life's easy for Cassandra. The privileged daughter of a rector, she's been protected from the extremist gangs who enforce the One Church's will.

Her boyfriend Ming is a bad influence, of course, with infidel parents who are constantly in trouble with the religious authorities. But Cass has no intention of letting their different backgrounds drive them apart.

Then they stumble across a corpse.

Whose corpse is it? How did it body end up in their secret childhood haunt? And is this person's death connected to other, older murders?

As the political atmosphere grows feverish, Cass realises she and Ming face extreme danger.

The scene is set for a murderously sinister dystopian satire.

Longlisted for the Royal Mail Awards for Scottish Books
Longlisted for the Lancashire Book of the Year Award
Longlisted for the Catalyst Book Award
2010 Carnegie Medal-nominated author

ISBN: 978-1-905537-08-2
RRP £6.99

See *www.stridentpublishing.co.uk* for details and a video trailer.

Janne Teller
nothing

NOTHING
Janne Teller

"Nothing matters."

"From the moment you are born, you start to die."

"The Earth is 4.6 billion years old. You'll live to be a maximum of one hundred. Life isn't worth the bother!"

So says Pierre Anthon when he decides that there is no meaning to life, leaves the classroom, climbs a plum tree, and stays there. His friends and classmates cannot get him to come down, not even by pelting him with rocks. So to prove to him that there is a meaning to life, they set out to build a heap of meaning in an abandoned sawmill.
But it soon becomes obvious that each person cannot give up what is most meaningful, so they begin to decide for one another what the others must give up. As the demands become more extreme, events begin to take a morbid turn.

A huge bestseller around the world, Nothing is about everything. It is a visionary, controversial, existential novel that has already a modern classic.

ISBN: 978-1-905537-32-7
RRP £7.99

See *www.stridentpublishing.co.uk* for details and a video trailer.